CALLED BACK

'THE DETECTIVE STORY CLUB is a clearing house for the best detective and mystery stories chosen for you by a select committee of experts. Only the most ingenious crime stories will be published under the THE DETECTIVE STORY CLUB imprint. A special distinguishing stamp appears on the wrapper and title page of every THE DETECTIVE STORY CLUB book—the Man with the Gun. Always look for the Man with the Gun when buying a Crime book.'

Wm. Collins Sons & Co. Ltd., 1929

Now the Man with the Gun is back in this series of COLLINS CRIME CLUB reprints, and with him the chance to experience the classic books that influenced the Golden Age of crime fiction.

▼▼▼▼▼▼▼▼▼▼▼▼▼▼▼▼▼▼

THE
DETECTIVE STORY
CLUB

LIST OF TITLES

THE PERFECT CRIME • ISRAEL ZANGWILL

THE MAYFAIR MYSTERY • FRANK RICHARDSON

THE MYSTERY OF THE SKELETON KEY • BERNARD CAPES

THE GRELL MYSTERY • FRANK FROËST

FURTHER TITLES IN PREPARATION

▲▲▲▲▲▲▲▲▲▲▲▲▲▲▲▲▲▲

CALLED BACK

A STORY OF CRIME BY
HUGH CONWAY

WITH AN INTRODUCTION BY
MARTIN EDWARDS

COLLINS
CRIME
CLUB

COLLINS CRIME CLUB
An imprint of HarperCollins*Publishers*
1 London Bridge Street
London SE1 9GF
www.harpercollins.co.uk

This edition 2015

1

First published in Great Britain by J. W. Arrowsmith 1883
Published by The Detective Story Club Ltd
for Wm Collins Sons & Co. Ltd 1929

Introduction © Martin Edwards 2015

A catalogue record for this book is
available from the British Library

ISBN 978-0-00-813711-3

Printed and bound in Great Britain by
Clays Ltd, St Ives plc

INTRODUCTION

CALLED BACK, Hugh Conway's most famous novel, was first published in 1883 as a 'Christmas annual' by a small Bristol publishing firm. The story rapidly earned such popular acclaim that 'many prophesied the displacement of Wilkie Collins by the new star', according to one of Collins' obituaries. Certainly, the book caused much more of a sensation than the first detective novel of a young Scottish writer four years later, *A Study in Scarlet*. Yet today, Conway's name is much less well-known than Wilkie Collins', let alone Arthur Conan Doyle's. So it is easy to forget that his reputation endured long after his premature death in 1885. *Called Back* entertained a later generation of readers when it was re-published in the Detective Story Club series in 1929, and was also filmed twice, in 1914 and 1933.

John Sutherland, an academic expert on Victorian fiction, has neatly summarised *Called Back* as a 'sensational novel of murder, amnesia, Siberian-exile, political assassination and detection'. Who could possibly resist such a confection? The main events of the story take place in the 1860s; they are recalled later by the narrator, Gilbert Vaughan, a respectable Englishman with a hatred of mysteries 'who has a romance hidden away beneath an outwardly prosaic life'.

At the age of 25, Vaughan is struck blind. Leaving his house in London one night, he becomes lost, and witnesses a mysterious killing. Confident that they cannot be recognised, the perpetrators allow him to escape with his life. Vaughan later recovers his sight and, on a trip to Italy, encounters a beautiful girl with whom he promptly falls in love. Their romance fails to progress, but he soon comes across her again in London, where he also meets Dr Manuel

Ceneri, who claims to be her uncle. Gradually, a dastardly scheme unfolds. Vaughan is not a wholly likeable man, but his persistence in his quest for the truth makes him a worthy protagonist. The long arm of coincidence reaches out time and again during the course of the narrative, prompting Vaughan's occasional exclamation: 'It was Fate!' But the book is written with Victorian verve.

The book rapidly sold more than a quarter of a million copies, making a fortune for its publisher, J. W. Arrowsmith. A paper-covered edition costing one shilling became the most renowned of the so-called 'shilling shockers' popular at the time. The story was also widely translated. Together with Joseph Comyns Carr, a prominent drama critic, theatre manager and playwright, Conway adapted the book for the stage, and long runs in both London and the provinces followed. There was even a burlesque version called *The Scalded Back!* Towards the end of her life, Emily Dickinson enjoyed reading the novel, which she described as 'a haunting story'; so taken was she with the phrase *Called Back* that it was added to her tombstone. *The Times* compared Stevenson's *Strange Case of Dr Jekyll and Mr Hyde* to *Called Back*, and while the reviewer admired Stevenson's story, he expressed doubt as to whether it would enjoy as much popular success as Conway's.

Conway threw himself into writing, with encouragement from Wilkie Collins himself, and his later books included two more 'Christmas annuals', notably the thriller *Dark Days*, which would also eventually feature in the Detective Story Club. His rise to fame had been meteoric, but sadly, it did not last. Having developed symptoms of TB, he travelled to the French Riviera to recuperate, but was diagnosed with typhoid fever, and died shortly afterwards at Monte Carlo, aged just 37. It is indicative of the literary status that he achieved in a short time that, after his death, Arrowsmiths asked an author as eminent as Wilkie Collins to write their next 'Christmas annual'; this resulted in *The Guilty River*, but it sold far less well than *Called Back*.

Conway's real name was Frederick John Fargus, and he was born in Bristol in 1848, the son of an auctioneer. Youthful enthusiasm for the novels of Captain Marryat inspired an ambition to become a sailor; his pseudonym came from *HMS Conway*, a frigate stationed in the river Mersey and used as a school ship for the training of aspiring naval officers, where he spent some of his formative years. An accident suffered on board the *Conway* damaged his hearing, and led Fargus to pursue a career in the family firm whilst trying to establish himself as an author. In 1879, he published a volume of poetry, and a collection of short stories appeared two years later. He showed signs of developing into an accomplished exponent of supernatural stories as well as thrillers, and after his death, Comyns Carr wrote to *The Times* extolling his gifts; in his view, *Called Back* barely hinted at Fargus' literary potential.

Who knows? It is not impossible that, had he lived and written for another two or three decades, Fargus would have ranked alongside such immortals as Collins, Stevenson, M.R. James and Conan Doyle. As a result of his untimely death, his legacy was less striking. Nonetheless, *Called Back* deserves to be read again, not merely as a reminder of an unfulfilled talent, but in its own right, as lively entertainment from a bygone age.

MARTIN EDWARDS
February 2015
www.martinedwardsbooks.com

CONTENTS

CHAPTER I

I HAVE a reason for writing this tale, or it would not become public property.

Once in a moment of confidence, I made a friend acquainted with some curious circumstances connected with one period of my life. I believe I asked him to hold his tongue about them—he says not. Anyway, he told another friend, with embellishments, I suspect; this friend told another, and so on and on. What the tale grew to at last I shall probably never learn; but since I was weak enough to trust my private affairs to another I have been looked upon by my neighbours as a man with a history—one who has a romance hidden away beneath an outwardly prosaic life.

For myself I should not trouble about this. I should laugh at the garbled versions of my story set floating about by my own indiscretion. It would matter little to me that one good friend has an idea that I was once a Communist and a member of the inner circle of a secret society—that another has heard that I have been tried on a capital charge—that another knows I was at one time a Roman Catholic, on whose behalf a special miracle was performed. If I were alone in the world and young, I dare say I should take no steps to still these idle rumours. Indeed, very young men feel flattered by being made objects of curiosity and speculation.

But I am not very young, nor am I alone. There is one who is dearer to me than life itself. One from whose heart, I am glad to say, every shadow left by the past is rapidly fading—one who only wishes to live her true sweet life without mystery or concealment—wishes to be thought neither better nor worse

1

than she really is. It is she who shrinks from the strange and absurd reports which are flying about as to our antecedents she who is vexed by those leading questions sometimes asked by inquisitive friends; and it is for her sake that I look up old journals, call back old memories of joy and grief, and tell everyone, who cares to read, all he can possibly wish to know, and, it may be, more than he has a right to know, of our lives. This done, my lips are sealed forever on the subject. My tale is here—let the inquisitive take his answer from it, not from me.

Perhaps, after all, I write this for my own sake as well. I also hate mysteries. One mystery which I have never been able to determine may have given me a dislike to everything which will not admit of an easy explanation.

To begin, I must go back more years than I care to enumerate; although I could, if necessary, fix the day and the year. I was young, just past twenty-five. I was rich, having when I came of age succeeded to an income of about two thousand a year; an income which, being drawn from the funds, I was able to enjoy without responsibility or anxiety as to its stability and endurance. Although since my twenty-first birthday I had been my own master, I had no extravagant follies to weigh me down, no debts to hamper me. I was without bodily ache or pain; yet I turned again and again on my pillow and said that my life for the future was a curse to me.

Had Death just robbed me of one who was dear to me? No; the only ones I had ever loved, my father and mother, had died years ago. Were my ravings those peculiar to an unhappy lover? No; my eyes had not yet looked with passion into a woman's eyes—and now would never do so. Neither Death nor Love made my lot seem the most miserable in the world.

I was young, rich, free as the wind to follow my own devices. I could leave England tomorrow and visit the most beautiful places on the earth: those places I had longed and determined to see. Now, I knew I should never see them, and I groaned in anguish at the thought.

My limbs were strong. I could bear fatigue and exposure. I could hold my own with the best walkers and the swiftest runners. The chase, the sport, the trial of endurance had never been too long or too arduous for me—I passed my left hand over my right arm and felt the muscles firm as of old. Yet I was as helpless as Samson in his captivity.

For, even as Samson, I was blind!

Blind! Who but the victim can even faintly comprehend the significance of that word? Who can *read* this and gauge the depth of my anguish as I turned and turned on my pillow and thought of the fifty years of darkness which might be mine—a thought which made me wish that when I fell asleep it might be to wake no more?

Blind! After hovering around me for years the demon of darkness had at last laid his hand upon me. After letting me, for a while, almost cheat myself into security, he had swept down upon me, folded me in his sable wings and blighted my life. Fair forms, sweet sights, bright colours, gay scenes mine no more! He claimed them all, leaving darkness, darkness, ever darkness! Far better to die, and, it may be, wake in a new world of light—'Better,' I cried in my despair, 'better even the dull red glare of Hades than the darkness of the world!'

This last gloomy thought of mine shows the state of mind to which I was reduced.

The truth is that, in spite of hope held out to me, I had resolved to be hopeless. For years I had felt that my foe was lying in wait for me. Often when gazing on some beautiful object, some fair scene, the right to enjoy which made one fully appreciate the gift of sight, a whisper seemed to reach my ear—'Some day I will strike again, then it will be all over.' I tried to laugh at my fears, but could never quite get rid of the presentiment of evil. My enemy had struck once—why not again?

Well I can remember his first appearance—his first attack. I remember a light-hearted schoolboy so engrossed in sport and study that he scarcely noticed how strangely dim the sight of one eye was getting, or the curious change which was taking place in its appearance. I remember the boy's father taking him to London, to a large dull-looking house in a quiet dull street. I remember our waiting in a room in which were several other people; most of whom had shades or bandages over their eyes. Such a doleful gathering it was that I felt much relieved when we were conducted to another room in which sat a kind, pleasant-spoken man, called by my father Mr Jay. This eminent man, after applying something which I know now was belladonna to my eyes, and which had the effect for a short time of wonderfully improving my sight, peered into my eyes by the aid of strong lenses and mirrors—I remember at the time wishing some of those lenses were mine—what splendid burning glasses they would make! Then he placed me with my back to the window and held a lighted candle before my face. All these proceedings seemed so funny that I was half inclined to laugh. My father's grave, anxious face alone restrained me from so doing. As soon as Mr Jay had finished his researches he turned to my father—

'Hold the candle as I held it. Let it shine into the right eye first. Now, Mr Vaughan, what do you see? How many candles, I mean?'

'Three—the one in the centre small and bright, but upside down.'

'Yes; now try the other eye. How many there?'

My father looked long and carefully.

'I can only see one,' he said, 'the large one.'

'This is called the catoptric test, an old-fashioned but infallible test, now almost superseded. The boy is suffering from lenticular cataract.'

This terribly sounding name took away all my wish to laugh. I glanced at my father and was surprised to notice his face wearing an expression of relief.

'That may be cured by an operation,' he said.

'Certainly; but in my judgment it is not well to meddle, so long as the other eye remains unaffected.'

'Is there danger?'

'There is always danger of the disease appearing in the sound eye; but, of course, it may not happen. Come to me at the first sign of such a thing. Good morning.'

The great specialist bowed us out, and I returned to my school life, troubling little about the matter, as it caused me no pain, and, although in less than a twelve-month the sight of one eye was completely obscured, I could see well enough for every purpose with the remaining one.

But I remembered every word of that diagnosis, although it was years before I recognized the importance of it. It was only when compelled by an accident to wear for some days a bandage over my sound eye that I realized the danger in which I stood, and from that moment felt that a merciless foe was ever waiting his time.

And now the time had come. In the first flush of my manhood, with all that one could wish for at my command, the foe had struck again.

He came upon me swiftly—far more swiftly than is his custom in such cases; yet it was long before I would believe the worst—long before I would confess to myself that my failing sight and the increasing fogginess of everything I looked at were due to more than a temporary weakness. I was hundreds of miles from home, in a country where travelling is slow. A friend being with me, I had no wish to make myself a nuisance by cutting our expedition short. So I said nothing for weeks, although at the end of each week my heart sank at the fresh and fearful advances made by the foe. At last, being unable to bear it, or in fact conceal it longer, I made known my condition to my comrade. We turned our faces homeward, and by the time London was reached and the long journey at an end, everything to me was blurred, dim, and obscured. I could just see, that was all!

I flew to the eminent oculist's. He was out of town. Had been ill, even at the point of death. He would not be back for two months, nor would he see any patient until his health was quite restored.

I had pinned my faith upon this man. No doubt there were as skilful oculists in London, Paris, or other capitals; but it was my fancy that, if I were to be saved, I could only be saved by Mr Jay. Dying men are allowed their whims: even the felon about to be hanged can choose his own breakfast, so I had an undoubted right to choose my own surgeon. I resolved to wait in darkness until Mr Jay returned to his duties. I was foolish. I had better have trusted myself in other clever hands. Before a month was over I had lost all hope, and at the end of six weeks I was almost distracted. Blind, blind, blind! I should be blind forever! So entirely had I lost heart that I began to think I would not have the operation performed at all. Why fly against fate? For the rest of my life I was doomed to darkness. The subtlest skill, the most delicate hand, the most modern appliances would never restore the light I have lost. For me the world was at an end.

Now that you know the cause, can you not imagine me, after weeks of darkness, broken in spirit, and, as I lay sleepless that night, almost wishing that the alternative refused by Job—to curse God and die—were mine? If you are unable to realize my condition, read the above to anyone who has lost his sight. He will tell you what his feelings were when the calamity first came upon him. He will understand the depths of I was not left entirely alone in my trouble. Like Job, I had comforters: but, unlike Eliphaz and Company, they were good-hearted fellows who spoke with cheerful conviction as to the certainty of my recovery. I was not so grateful for these visits as I should have been. I hated the thought of anyone seeing me in my helpless condition. Day by day my frame of mind grew more and more desponding and morbid.

My best friend of all was a humble one: Priscilla Drew, an old and trusted servant of my mother's. She had known me from earliest childhood. When I returned to England I could not bear the thought of trusting my helpless self entirely to a stranger's care, so I wrote to her and begged her to come to me. I could at least groan and lament before her without feeling shame. She came, wept over me for a while, and then, like a sensible woman, bestirred herself to do all she could to mitigate the hardships of my lot. She found comfortable lodgings, installed her troublesome charge therein, and day and night was ever at his beck and call. Even now, as I lay awake and tossing in mental anguish, she was sleeping on an extemporized bed just outside the folding doors, which opened from my bedroom to the sitting-room.

It was a stifling night in August. The sluggish air which crept in through the open window made little perceptible difference in the temperature of my room. Everything seemed still, hot, and dark. The only sound I could hear was the regular breathing of the sleeper behind the door, which she had left an inch or two ajar in order that she might catch my faintest call. I had gone early to bed. What had I to wait up for now? It was sleep and sleep alone which brought forgetfulness, but tonight sleep refused to come to me. I struck my repeater. I had bought one in order that I might at least know the time. The little bell told me it was just past one o'clock. Craving for sleep I sighed and sank back upon my pillow.

Presently a sudden fierce longing to be out of doors came over me. It was night—very few people would be about. There was a broad pavement in front of the row of houses in one of which I lodged. Up and down this I might walk in perfect safety. Even if I only sat on the doorstep it would be better than lying in this close hot room, tossing from side to side unable to sleep.

The desire took such full possession of me that I was on the point of calling old Priscilla and making her aware of it; but knowing she was sleeping soundly, I hesitated. I had been unusually restless, cross, and exacting during the day, and my old nurse—heaven reward her!—was serving me for love, not for money. Why should I disturb her? Let me begin to learn to help myself like others in my wretched plight. I had already acquired this much, to dress without assistance. If I could now do this and leave the room unheard, I could, I felt sure, grope my way to the front door, let myself out, and, whenever I chose, return by the aid of the latchkey. The thought of even a temporary independence was attractive, and my spirits rose as I resolved to make the attempt.

I crept softly from my bed and slowly, but easily dressed myself, hearing all the while the sleeper's regular breathing. Then, cautious as a thief, I stole to the door which led from my bedroom to the landing. I opened it without noise and stood on the thick carpet outside, smiling as I thought of the sleeper's dismay if she awoke and discovered my absence. I closed the door, then, guiding myself by the balustrade, passed lightly down the stairs and reached the street door without accident.

There were other lodgers in the house, among them young men who came in at all hours, so, the door being always left on the latch, I had no bolts to contend with. In a moment I was on the doorstep, with the door behind me closed.

I stood for a short time irresolute, almost trembling at my temerity. This was the first time I had ventured beyond the house without a guiding hand to trust to. Yet I knew there was nothing to fear. The street—a quiet one—was deserted. The pavement was broad, I could walk up and down without let or hindrance, guiding myself, after the manner of other blind persons, by tapping my stick against the curbstone or the railings Still I must take a few precautions to enable me to ascertain my latitude and longitude at will.

I came down the four steps which led from the front door, turned myself to the right, and, by aid of the line of railings, set my face toward the end of the street. Then I began to walk and to count my steps, sixty-two of which brought my right foot on to a road, which told me I had reached my limit. I turned, counted back the sixty-two paces, and then sixty-five more in the same direction before I found myself again off the pavement. My calculations were verified by my knowing that my house was very nearly in the centre of the row. I was now quite at my ease; I had determined the length of my tether; I could walk up and down the deserted street, yet, at any time I wished to do so, could, by counting from either end, arrest my steps in front of my abode.

So, mightily proud of my success, for a while I went up and down—up and down. I heard one or two cabs pass me, and also one or two persons afoot. As these latter seemed to pay no attention to me, I felt glad to think that my appearance and gait were not such as to attract notice. Most men like to conceal their infirmities.

This night excursion did me a great deal of good. Perhaps it was finding that I was not altogether so helpless and dependent that changed in a few minutes my whole frame of mind. The mental rebound took place. I went from despondency to hope—extravagant hope—even to certainty. Like a revelation it came to me that my malady was curable; that, in spite of my presentiment, what friends had been assuring me would prove to be the truth. So elated I grew that I threw my head back and walked with a firm quick step, almost forgetting that I was sightless. I began to think of many things, and my thoughts were happier ones than I had known for months. I gave up counting my paces, I walked on and on, planning what I should do; where I should go when my darkness was removed. I do not know whether I may have at times guided myself by the wall or pavement edge; but if so I did it mechanically and instinctively, without noticing the action or remembering it afterward.

I cannot say whether it may be possible for a blind man, who can divest himself of the fear of encountering unseen obstacles, to walk as straightly and accurately as one who can see. I only know that, in my preoccupied and elevated state of mind, I must have done so. Intoxicated and carried away by the return of hope, I may have walked as a somnambulist or as one in a trance. Anyway, forgetful of all save my brighter thoughts, I went on and on, heedless of the missing sense, until coming full against a person walking in the opposite direction recalled me from my visions and brought me back to my misery. I felt the man I had encountered shake himself free; I heard him mutter 'stupid fool!' and go swiftly on his way, leaving me motionless on the spot where the collision had occurred, wondering where I was and what I should do.

It was no use attempting to find my way back unaided. Not having brought my repeater with me I could not even say how long I had been walking. It might have been ten minutes, it might have been an hour since I gave up counting my steps. Judging by the number of things I had thought of since that rapturous exaltation of mind commenced it seemed more likely to be the latter. Now that I had come back to the earth I must be content to remain on this particular spot of it until I heard the step of a policeman or someone else who might happen to be abroad at this unusual hour—unusual, at least in this quiet part of London. I leaned my back against the wall and waited patiently.

I soon heard an approaching step; but such a staggering, uncertain, lurching kind of step, that from the sound of the feet alone I was able to determine the condition of their owner, and was obliged to decide that he was not the man I wanted. I must let him pass and wait for another. But the feet staggered up to me and stopped near me, whilst a voice, jolly, but like the feet unsteady, cried—

"'Nother feller worsh than me! Can't get on at all—eh, old chap? Comfort t' think someone's head 'll ache worsh than mine tomorrow!'

'Can you tell me the way to Walpole Street?' I asked, standing erect to show him I was sober.

'Walpole Street—course I can—closhe by—third to left, I think.'

'If you are going that way would you lead me to the corner of it. Unhappily I am blind and have lost my way.'

'Blind, poor beggar—not screwed then. Guess I'm in nice state to lead anyone. Blind leading blind—both tumble into ditch. I shay, though,' he added with drunken gravity, 'make a bargain—I lend you eyes, you lend me legsh. Good idea Come 'long.'

He took my arm and we went yawing up the street. Presently he stopped.

'Walpole Street,' he hiccuped. 'Shall I take you to your house?'

'No, thank you. Please put my hand on the railing of the corner house. I shall be all right then.'

'Wish I were all right. Wish I could borrow your legs to take me home,' said my bibulous conductor. 'Good night— Blesh you.'

I heard him tack away, then turned to complete my journey.

I was not quite certain as to which end of Walpole Street I was starting from; that mattered little. Either sixty-two or sixty-five paces would leave me in front of my door. I counted sixty-two, and then felt for the entrance between the railings; not finding it, I went on a step or two until I came to it. I was glad to have reached home without accident, and, to tell the truth, was beginning to feel a little ashamed of my escapade. I hoped that Priscilla had not discovered my absence and alarmed the house, and I trusted I should be able to regain my room as quietly as I had quitted it. With all my elaborate calculations, I was not quite sure that I had hit upon the right house; but if they were incorrect I could only be a door or two away from it, and the key in my hand would be a certain test. I went up the doorsteps—was it four or five I had counted as I came out? I fumbled for the keyhole and inserted the latchkey. It turned easily, and the door opened. I had not made a mistake. I felt an inward glow of satisfaction at having hit upon the house at the first attempt. 'It must have been a blind man who first discovered that Necessity is the mother of Invention,' I said, as I softly closed the door behind me and prepared to creep up to my own room. I wondered what the time was. All I knew was that it must be still night, for I was able to distinguish light from darkness. As I had found myself so close to Walpole Street I could not have walked for any length of time in my ecstatic state, so I fancied it must be somewhere about two o'clock.

Even more anxious than when I started to make no noise which might awaken people, I found the bottom of the staircase and began my stealthy ascent.

Somehow, blind as I was, the place seemed unfamiliar to me. The balustrade I was touching did not seem the same. The very texture of the carpet under my feet seemed different. Could it be possible that I had entered the wrong house? There are plenty of instances on record of a key having opened a strange lock. Could I, through such a circumstance, have strayed into a neighbour's house? I paused; the perspiration rising on my brow as I thought of the awkward situation in which I should be placed if it were so. For a moment I resolved to retrace my steps and try the next house; but I could not be quite sure I was wrong. Then I remembered that in my own house a bracket, with a plaster figure upon it, hung near the top of the stairs. I knew the exact place, having been cautioned many times to keep my head by going on and feeling for this landmark; so on I went.

I ran my fingers softly along the wall, but no bracket could I find. My hand touched the lintel of a door instead. Then I knew, for certain, I was in the wrong house. The only thing to be done was to creep out as quietly as I had entered and try my luck next door. As I turned to grope my way back I heard the murmur of voices—late as it was, there were people talking in the room, the door of which my fingers had so lightly touched.

I could not distinguish words, but I was sure the voices were those of men. I stood irresolute. Would it not be better to knock at the door and throw myself upon the mercy of the inmates of the room? I could apologize and explain. My blindness would account for the mistake. Someone would, no doubt, be kind enough to put me on my right road home. Yes, this was the best thing to do. I could not go on creeping into strange houses like a midnight thief. Perhaps each house in the row had an equally common lock and my key might open all. If so, the end would be that some alarmed householder would put a bullet into me before I had time to assert my innocence.

Just as I raised my fingers to tap at the door I heard another voice—a woman's voice. It seemed to come from the back room and was singing to an accompaniment played softly on a piano. I paused and listened—

I have been so occupied with complaining of the hardship of my lot I have not told you I had one solace to my misery; that merciful gift, so often bestowed on the blind, music. Had it not been for this I believe those weeks of darkness and uncertainty would have driven me mad. Had it not been that I could pass many weary hours away playing to myself, that I could be taken to concerts and hear others play and sing, my days would have been unbearable, and I shudder to think of what aid I might have called in to render them less burdensome.

I waited and listened to the song. It was taken from an opera recently produced on the Continent, an opera not yet popularly known in England, and the song was one that few amateurs would dare to attempt. The singer, whoever she might be, sang it softly and under her voice, as though fearing to throw it out with full force. The lateness of the hour might well account for this restraint. Nevertheless, anyone capable of judging must have known he was listening to no ordinary singer. It was easy to recognize the trained skill and dormant power, and imagine what, under favourable circumstances, that voice might accomplish. I was enchanted. My idea was that I had stumbled into a nest of professionals—people whose duties ended so late, that to enjoy any evening at all, night must be greatly encroached upon. All the better for me! Bohemians themselves, my unexpected nocturnal intrusion might not frighten them out of their wits.

The singer had now commenced the second verse. I placed my ear close to the door to catch every note. I was curious to hear what she would make of the effective but trying finale, when—oh horrible contrast to the soft sweet liquid notes and subdued words of passionate love!—I heard a gasp, a spasmodic, fearful gasp, that could convey but one meaning. I heard it succeeded by a long deep groan, which terminated in a gurgling sound which froze my blood. I heard the music stop suddenly, and the cry, the piercing cry of a woman ring out like a frightful change from melody to discord, and then I heard a dull heavy thud on the floor!

I waited to hear no more. I knew that some dreadful deed had been perpetrated within a few feet of where I stood. My heart beat wildly and fiercely. In the excitement of the moment I forgot that I was not like others—forgot that strength and courage could avail me nothing—forgot everything save a desire to prevent the accomplishment of crime—the wish to do a man's duty in saving life and succouring the ones in peril. I threw open the door and rushed headlong into the room. Then, as I became aware of the presence of strong light, but light which revealed nothing to me, the folly and rashness of my proceedings came fully home to me, and like a flash it crossed my mind that unarmed, blind and helpless, I had rushed into that room to meet my death.

I heard an oath—an exclamation of surprise. In the distance I heard the cry of the woman, but it sounded muffled and faint; it seemed to me that a struggle was going on in that part of the room. Powerless though I was to aid, I turned impulsively and took a couple of steps in the direction whence the cry came; my foot caught in something and I fell prostrate on the body of a man. Even in the midst of the horror that awaited me I shuddered as I felt my hand, lying on the fallen man, grow wet with some warm fluid which slowly trickled over it.

Before I could rise strong muscular living hands were upon my throat, holding me down, whilst a short distance off I heard the sharp click of a pistol lock. Oh, for a light for a second! If only to see those who were about to take my life, if only—strange fancy—to know in what part of me to expect the fatal bullet And I, who some hour or two ago lay and dared to wish for death, felt at this moment that life, even my darkened life, was as dear to me as to any creature under the sun. So, I cried aloud, and my voice sounded to me like the voice of a stranger—

'Spare me! I am blind! blind! blind!'

CHAPTER II

DRUNK OR DREAMING

THE hands pinning me down did not for an instant relax their grasp; yet they might safely have done so. Situated as I was I felt that my only chance of life was to lie still and convince, if I could, the persons in that room of the truth of my assertion. Nothing could be gained, but everything would be lost by resistance. I was strong, but, even if all the senses had been mine, I doubted if I could compete successfully with the man who held me down. I could feel the nervous power of his hands and arms. Certainly, now that I was blind and helpless, the struggle would be a short one. Besides, he had companions, how many I knew not, ready to help him. The first movement I made would be the end of everything so far as I was concerned.

I made no further attempt to rise, but lay as still and un-resisting as the prostrate form across which I had fallen. Every moment seemed an hour!

Think of my situation. A blind man in a strange room in a strange house—held down on the body of a man whose last groan he had just heard—held down and at the mercy of those who it was certain had just taken part in a black and cowardly crime! Unable to look into the faces of the murderers around him and learn whether their looks meant life or death to him! Expecting every moment to feel the sharp stab of a knife or the fiery sting of a bullet! Seeing nothing and feeling nothing save the hands upon his throat and the dead body beneath him! Even hearing nothing save that stifled moaning in the distance! Can the wildest flights of fiction show a parallel to my case?

Since that night I have quite disbelieved in the possibility of people's hair turning suddenly grey. If such a thing can be I must have left that room with the locks of an old man.

I can only say that even now as, after the lapse of years, I write this; even as I see everything around me safe, still, and at peace; even though I know the ones I love are close at hand, my pen trembles, my blood feels chilled, and a faintness steals over me as the recollection of the most terrible moments in my life comes to me with a vividness I cannot describe. It was well for me that I could keep still and cry again and again, 'I am blind—look and see!' My quiescence, the tone of my voice, may have turned the balance on which my life hung—may have carried conviction to my hearers. Presently the strong light of a lamp was perceptible to my obscured vision; a lamp placed so close to me that I could feel its hot glow upon my face; and I was aware that someone was stooping or kneeling down and peering into my eyes. His breath struck against my cheek: a short, quick, excited breath—how could it be otherwise after the deed in which he had just taken part?

At last he rose; a moment afterward the restraining hands moved from me, and then, for the first time, I began to hope that my life might be spared.

As yet none of those around me had spoken. Now I heard voices, but whispering so softly that even my sharpened ears could not catch the purport of a single word, although I could gather that three persons at least were engaged in that hushed consultation.

All the while, like a dreary and fitting accompaniment, I could hear that stifled moaning—a woman's moaning. I would have given all I possessed—all save life—in exchange for a minute's sight, that I might have been able to comprehend what had passed and what was passing around me.

Still the whispers continued. They came thick and fast, running into and interrupting each other, as from men in hot but guarded discussion. It needed little intelligence to guess the subject of that debate! Presently they died away altogether, and, for a time, the only sound I heard was that terrible, muffled moan—that continued with a dreary monotony.

A foot touched me. 'You may stand up,' I heard someone say. When I burst so recklessly into the room I fancied the exclamation with which I was greeted came from foreign lips, but the man who now addressed me spoke in pure English. By this time I was beginning to recover self-possession and was able to make a mental note of these facts.

Thankful at being allowed to quit my ghastly couch, I rose. As I could think of nothing better to do I stood motionless.

'Walk this way—straight on—four paces,' said the voice. I obeyed. The third step brought me in collision with the wall. No doubt this was an extra test as to the truth of my statement.

A hand was placed upon my shoulder and I was guided to a chair. 'Now, sir,' said the speaker who had before addressed me, 'tell us, in as few words as possible, who you are—how and why you came here. Be quick, we have no time to spare.'

I well knew they had no time to spare. They had much to do—much to hide. Oh, for the gift of sight for one moment! I would purchase it, even if the price were years of darkness!

Shortly and simply as I could, I told them what had brought me into such straits. The only thing I concealed was my true name. Why should these assassins know it? If I revealed it they might set a watch upon me and at any moment their safety demanded it I might share the fate of him who lay within a few feet of my chair. So I gave a fictitious name, but everything else I told them was true.

All the while I was speaking I heard that distressing sound at the other end of the room. It drove me nearly mad. I believe, could I have made sure of reaching through my darkness and catching one of those men by the throat, with the certainty of crushing life out of him, I should have done so, even had such an act sealed my own fate.

When my explanation was over another whispered consultation took place. Then the spokesman demanded the key which had so nearly cost me my life. I suppose they tried it and found it acted as I said. It was not returned to me, but I heard the voice once more.

'Fortunately for you we have decided to believe your tale. Stand up.' I did so and was led to another part of the room and again placed in a chair. As, after the manner of the blind, I stretched out my hands, I found I was in a corner of the room, my face turned to the angle of the walls.

'If you move or look around,' said the voice, 'our belief in your blindness will vanish.'

It was impossible to misunderstand the grim threat conveyed by the last words. I could only sit quiet and listen with all my ears.

Yes, they had much to do. They moved about busily and rapidly. I heard cupboards and drawers opened. I detected the sound of papers being torn and the smell of papers burning. I heard them raise some dead weight from the floor—heard a sound as of rent cloth and linen—heard the jingle of money, even the tick of a watch as it was drawn forth from somewhere and laid on the table near me. Then I felt a breath of air and knew that the door had been opened. I heard heavy footsteps on the stairs—the steps of men bearing a weighty burden, and I shuddered as I thought what that burden must be.

Before the last task was completed the woman's moan had ceased. For some time it had been growing fainter and only sounding at recurring intervals. Now I heard it no longer. This cessation was a great relief to my overwrought nerves, but my heart grew sick as I thought it may be there were two victims instead of one.

Although at least two men must have borne that weight away, I knew I was not left alone. I heard someone throw himself into a chair with a half weary sigh and guessed he had been left to guard me. I was longing to make my escape—longing to wake and find I had been dreaming. The suspense or the nightmare was growing unbearable. I said, without turning my head, 'How long am I to be kept amid these horrors?'

I heard the man move in his chair, but he made no answer. 'May I not go?' I pleaded. 'I have seen nothing. Put me out into the street—anywhere. I shall go mad if I stay here longer.'

Still no answer. I said no more.

By and by the absent men returned to their companion. I heard the door close after them. Then came more whispers, and I heard the drawing of a cork and the jingle of glasses. They were refreshing themselves after the night's dark work.

Presently a curious odour—that of some drug—was perceptible. A hand was laid on my shoulder and a glass full of some liquid was placed between my fingers.

'Drink,' said the voice—the only voice I had heard.

'I will not,' I cried, 'it may be poison.'

I heard a short harsh laugh and felt a cold metallic ring laid against my forehead.

'It is not poison; it is an opiate and will do you no harm. But this,' and as he spoke I felt the pressure of the little iron circlet, 'this is another affair. Choose!'

I drained the glass and was glad to feel the pistol moved from my head. 'Now,' said the spokesman, taking the empty glass from my hand, 'if you are a wise man, when you awake tomorrow you will say, "I have been drunk or dreaming." You have heard us but not seen us, but remember we know you.'

He left me and in a short time, do what I would to struggle against it, heavy drowsiness came over me. Thoughts grew incoherent and reason seemed leaving me. My head fell first on one side, then on the other. The last thing I can remember is a strong arm encircling me and keeping me from tumbling out of my chair. Whatever the drug was, its action was strong and swift.

For hours and hours it held me senseless, and when at last its power faded and my mind, struggling back to a clouded sort of consciousness, made, after many attempts, the fact apparent to me that I was lying on a bed, and, moreover, as I found by stretching out my arms and feeling around, my own bed, is it to be wondered at that I said to myself, 'I have dreamed the most frightful dream that ever came to a tormented mind'? After this effort of mind I sank back once more in a semi-conscious state, but fully persuaded I had never quitted my bed. My relief at this discovery was immense.

Yet if my mind grew easy, I cannot say the same for the body. My head seemed preparing to split in two; my tongue was dry and parched. These unpleasant facts became more and more noticeable as consciousness gradually returned. I sat up in the bed and pressed my hands to my throbbing brows.

'Oh, dear heart!' I heard my old nurse say. 'He is coming round at last.' Then another voice—a man's voice, soft and bland.

'Yes, your master will soon be well again. Kindly let me feel your pulse, Mr Vaughan.'

A soft finger was laid upon my wrist.

'Who is it?' I asked.

'I am Doctor Deane, at your service,' said the stranger.

'Have I been ill? How long? How many days?'

'A few hours only. There is nothing to be alarmed at. Lie down again and keep quiet for a while. Are you thirsty?'

'Yes, I am dying with thirst—give me water.'

They did so. I drank greedily, and felt somewhat relieved.

'Now, nurse,' I heard the doctor say, 'make him some weak tea, and when he wants anything to eat let him have it. I will look in again later on.'

Doctor Deane was shown out, and old Priscilla, returning to my bedside, patted and punched the pillows to make me more comfortable. By this time I was wide awake and the experiences of the night were coming back to me with a distinctness and detail far above those of a recalled dream.

'What is the time?' I asked.

'Nigh upon noon, Master Gilbert.' Priscilla spoke in a sorrowful, injured manner.

'Noon! what has been the matter with me?'

The old servant was weeping. I could hear her. She made no answer, so I repeated my question.

'Oh, Master Gilbert!' she sobbed, 'how could you do it? When I came into the room and saw the empty bed I thought I should have dropped.'

When she saw the empty bed! I trembled. The horrors of the night were real!

'How could you do it, Master Gilbert?' continued Priscilla. 'To go out without a word, and wander half over London, all alone and not able to see a thing!'

'Sit down and tell me what you mean—what has happened.'

She had not yet quite aired her grievance. 'If you wanted to get tipsy or to take any of them stuffs to send you to sleep and make you insensible, you might have done it at home, Master Gilbert. I shouldn't have minded once in a way.'

'You're a kind old fool, Priscilla Tell me all about last night.'

It was not until she saw I was getting quite angry that her tongue would consent to run pretty straight, and when I heard her account of what had occurred my head was whirling. This is what she told me.

It must have been about an hour after my stealthy exit that she awoke. She put her ear to the door to make certain that I was asleep and wanting nothing. Hearing no sound of life in my room she entered it, and found the bed untenanted and me gone. Probably she was even more frightened than she owned to being. She knew all about my despondency and complainings of the last few days, and I have no doubt but her first fear was that I had destroyed myself. She started in search of me, and at once recognizing the impossibility of finding me without assistance, turned to that first and last resource of an Englishwoman in such a difficulty—the police.

Having told her tale at the nearest station, and by entreaties, and by enlarging on my infirmity, made known the urgency of the case, and secured sympathy, telegraphic messages were sent, to other police stations asking if any one answering to my description had been found. Priscilla waited upon thorns until about five o'clock in the morning, when a reply came from the other end of the town. It stated that a young man who appeared to be blind, and who was certainly drunk and incapable, had just been brought in.

Priscilla flew to the rescue. She found me lying senseless, and destined, upon my recovery, to be brought before the magistrate. A doctor was soon procured, who testified to my innocence so far as alcohol was concerned. The energetic Priscilla, after placing me safely in a cab, gave the officers a bit of her mind as to the discomforts under which she a found me labouring. She then departed triumphantly with her unconscious charge, and laid him on the bed he had so rashly quitted.

I am grieved to be compelled to gather from her words that, in spite of the indignation she displayed toward the policemen, her estimate of my condition was the same as theirs. She was particularly grateful to the doctor, whom, I fear, she looked upon as a clever and complaisant practitioner, who had extricated a gentleman from a scrape by a well-timed but untruthful explanation.

'But I never knew a body stop insensible so long after it. Don't ee do it again, Master Gilbert,' she concluded.

I did not combat her suspicions. Priscilla was scarcely the one to whom I wished to confide the adventures of the night. By far the simplest way was to say nothing, to leave her to draw her own and, perhaps, not unnatural conclusions.

'I won't do it again,' I said. 'Now get me some breakfast. Tea and toast—anything.'

She went to do my bidding. It was not that I was hungry. I wanted to be alone for a few minutes, to think—or think as well as my aching head would allow.

I recalled everything that had happened since I left the door of my house. The entranced walk, the drunken guide, the song I had heard, and, afterward, those horrible, eloquent sounds and touches. Everything was clear and connected up to the moment the opiate was forced upon me; after that my mind was blank. Priscilla's tale showed me that during that blank I must have been transported several miles and deposited in the thoroughfare where I was found by the policeman. I saw through the crafty scheme. I had been dropped, insensible, far away from the scene of the crime at which I had been present. How wild and improbable my tale would seem. Would anyone believe it?

Then I remembered my horror at what I felt streaming over my hand as I lay pinned down upon the fallen man. I called Priscilla.

'Look,' I said, holding my right hand toward her, 'is it clean—was it clean when you found me?'

'Clean—la, no, Master Gilbert!'

'What was on it?' I asked, excitedly.

'All covered with mud, just as if you'd been dabbling in the gutter. The first thing I did when I got you home was to wash your poor hands and face. I hoped it would bring you round—it generally does, you know.'

'But my coat sleeve—my shirt sleeve. The right hand side. See if anything is on them.'

Priscilla laughed. 'You haven't got ne'er a right-hand sleeve left. They were cut or torn off above the elbow. Your arm was naked.'

Every scrap of circumstantial evidence which would confirm my tale was vanishing away. There would be nothing to support it except the assertion of a blind man, who left his house in the dead of night, secretly, and who was found, several hours afterward, miles away, in such a state that the guardians of the public morals were compelled to take charge of him.

Yet I could not remain silent with the knowledge of such a crime weighing on my mind. The next day I had entirely recovered from the effects of the opiate, and after consideration sent for my solicitor. He was a confidential friend, and I resolved to be guided by his advice. In a very short time I found it was hopeless to think of carrying conviction to his mind. He listened gravely, giving vent to 'Well, well!' 'Bless my soul!' 'Shocking!' and other set expressions of surprise, but I knew he was only humouring me, and looked upon the whole thing as a delusion. I have no doubt that Priscilla had been talking to him and telling him all she knew. His incredulity annoyed me, so I told him, testily, I should say no more about the affair.

'Well, I wouldn't if I were you,' he said.

'You don't believe me?'

'I believe you are saying what you think is true; but if you ask me, my opinion is that you walked in your sleep and dreamed all this.'

Too cross to argue with him, I took his advice, so far as he was concerned, and said no more about it. Afterwards I tried another friend with a similar result. If those who had known me from childhood would not believe me, how could I expect strangers to do so?

Everything I had to reveal was so vague and unsupported. I could not even fix upon the spot where the crime was committed. I had ascertained that no house in Walpole Street could be opened by a key similar to mine. There was no other street of that name anywhere near. My friend with the unsteady feet must have misunderstood me and conducted me to another row of houses.

I thought, at one time, of advertising and asking him to communicate with me, but I could not word a request which should be intelligible to him, without, perchance, exciting the suspicions of those who were concerned in the crime. Even now, if they had discovered my true name and abode, there might be someone on the watch for any movement I might make. I had been spared once, but no mercy would be shown me a second time. Why should I risk my life by making disclosures which would not be believed—accusations against men who were unknown to me? What good could I do? By now the assassins must have hidden all trace of the crime, and made good their retreat. Why should I face the ridicule which must attach to such a tale as mine, the truth of which I could not prove? No; let the horrors of that night be as a dream. Let them fade and be forgotten.

Soon I have something else to think of; something that may well drive such dismal memories from my mind. Hope has become certainty. I am almost delirious with delight. Science has triumphed! My defeated foe has left me. I am told his return is almost beyond possibility. The world is light again! I can see.

But my cure was a long and tedious affair. Both eyes were operated upon. First one, and, when the success of that operation was assured, the other. It was months before I was allowed to emerge altogether from darkness. Light was doled out to me sparingly and cautiously. What did that matter so long that I knew there was light again for me? I was patient, very patient and grateful. I followed Mr Jay's instructions to the letter, knowing I should reap the reward of so doing.

My case bad been treated by the simplest and safest method of operation—the one which is always chosen when the nature of the disease and the age of the patient permits—solution or absorption it is termed. When it was all over, and all danger of inflammation at an end; when I found that by the aid of strong convex glasses I could see well enough for all ordinary purposes, Mr Jay congratulated both himself and me. It promised, he said, to be the most thoroughly successful cure he had ever taken part in. It must have been something above the common, as I am informed that every book on the eye which has since been published cites my case as an example of what may be done.

Not until my dying day shall I forget that time when my cure was declared a fact; when the bandages were removed, and I was told I might now use, sparingly, my uncurtained eyes.

The joy, from what seemed never-ending night, to wake and see the sun, the stars—the clouds sped by the wind across the fair blue sky! To see green branches swaying with the breeze, and throwing trembling shadows on my path! To mark the flower; a bud but yesterday—today a bloom! To watch the broad bright sea grow splendid with the crimson of the west! To gaze on pictures, people, mountains, streams—to know shape, colour, form and tint! To see, not hear alone, the moving lips and laugh of those who grasped my hand and spoke kind words!

To me, in those first days of new-born light, the face of every woman, man, and child seemed welcome as the face of some dear friend, long lost and found again!

After this description of my ecstasy it seems pure bathos to say that the only thing which detracted from it was my being obliged to wear those strong convex glasses. I was young, and they were horribly disfiguring.

'Shall I never be able to do without them?' I asked, rather ruefully.

'That,' replied Mr Jay, 'is a point upon which I wish to speak to you. You will never be able to do without *glasses*. Remember, I have destroyed, absorbed, dissolved the glasses in your eyes called crystalline lenses. Their place is now supplied by the fluid humour. This has a high refracting power. Very often if you don't give in to Nature she will give in to you. If you can take the trouble to coerce her, she will gradually meet you. If anyone should do this, it is you. You are young; you have no profession, and your bread does not depend upon your sight. Glasses you must always wear, but if you insist that Nature shall act without such strong aids as these, the chances are she will at last consent to do so. It is a tedious process: few have been able or have had patience to persevere; but my experience is that in many instances it may be done.'

I determined it should be done. I followed his advice. At great personal inconvenience I wore glasses which only permitted me to say I could see at all. But my reward came. Slowly, very slowly, I found my sight growing stronger, till, in about two years' time, I could, by the aid of glasses, the convexity of which was so slight as to be scarcely noticeable, see as well as most of my fellow-creatures. Then I began once more to enjoy life.

I cannot say that, during those two years spent in perfecting my cure, I thought no more about that terrible night; but I made no further attempt to unravel the mystery, or to persuade any one that I had not imagined those events. I buried the history of my adventure in my heart, and never again spoke of it. In case of need, I wrote down all the particulars, and then tried to banish all memory of what I had heard. I succeeded fairly well except for one thing. I could not for any long period keep my thoughts from the remembrance of that woman's moaning—that pitiable transition of the voice from sweet melody to hopeless despair. It was that cry which troubled my dreams, if ever I dreamed of that night—it was that cry which rang in my ears as I woke, trembling, but thankful to find that this time, at least, I was only dreaming.

CHAPTER III

THE FAIREST SIGHT OF ALL

IT is spring—the beautiful spring of Northern Italy. My friend Kenyon and I are lounging about in the rectangular city of Turin, as happy and idle a pair of comrades as may anywhere be met with. We have been here a week, long enough to do all the sight-seeing demanded by duty. We have seen San Giovanni and the churches. We have toiled, or beasts of burden have toiled with us, up La Superga, where we have gazed at the mausoleum of Savoy's princely line. We have seen enough of the cumbrous old Palazzo Madama, which frowns at our hotel across the Piazzi Castello. We have marvelled at the plain, uninteresting looking Palazzo Reale, and our mirth has been moved by the grotesque brick-work decoration of the Palazzo Carignano. We have criticised the rather poor picture gallery. In fact we have done Turin thoroughly, and with contempt bred by familiarity, are ceasing to feel like pitiful little atoms as we stand in the enormous squares and crane our necks looking at Marochetti's immense bronze statues.

Our tasks are over. We are now simply loafing about and enjoying ourselves; revelling in the delicious weather, and trying to make up our languid but contented minds as to when we shall leave the town and where our next resting place shall be.

We wander down the broad Via di Po, lingering now and then to peer into the enticing shops which lurk in its shady arcades; we pass through the spacious Piazzi Vittorio Emanuele; we cross the bridge whose five granite arches span the classic Po; we turn opposite the domed church and

soon are walking up the wide shaded path which leads to the
Capuchin Monastery; the broad terrace in front of which is our
favourite haunt. Here we can lounge and see the river at our
feet, the great town stretching from its further bank, the open
plain beyond the town, and, far, far away in the background,
the glorious snow-capped Alps, with Monte Rosa and Grand
Paradis towering above their brothers. No wonder we enjoy the
view from this terrace more than churches, palaces, or pictures.

We gaze our fill, and then retrace our steps and saunter
back as lazily as we came. After lingering a few moments
at our hotel some hazy destination prompts us to cross the
great square, past the frowning old castle, leads us up the
Via di Seminario, and we find ourselves for the twentieth
time in front of San Giovanni. I stop with my head in the
air admiring what architectural beauties its marble front can
boast, and as I am trying to discover them am surprised to
hear Kenyon announce his intention of entering the building

'But we have vowed a vow,' I said, 'that the interior of
churches, picture galleries, and other tourist traps shall know
us no more.'

'What makes the best of men break their vows?'

'Lots of things, I suppose.'

'But one thing in particular. Whilst you are staring up at
pinnacles and buttresses, and trying to look as if you knew
architecture as well as Ruskin, the fairest of all sights, a
beautiful woman, passes right under your nose.'

'I understand—I absolve you.'

'Thank you. She went into the church. I feel devotional,
and will go too.'

'But our cigars?'

'Chuck them to the beggars. Beware of miserly habits,
Gilbert; they grow on one.'

Knowing that Kenyon was not the man to abandon a choice
Havana without a weighty reason, I did as he suggested and
followed him into the dim cool shades of San Giovanni.

No service was going on. The usual little parties of sight-seers were walking about and looking much impressed as beauties they could not comprehend were being pointed out to them. Dotted about here and there were silent worshippers. Kenyon glanced round eagerly in quest of 'the fairest of all sights', and after a while discovered her.

'Come this way,' he said; 'let us sit down and pretend to be devout Catholics. We can catch her profile here.'

I placed myself next to him, and saw, a few seats from us, an old Italian woman kneeling and praying fervently, whilst in a chair at her side sat a girl of about twenty-two.

A girl who might have belonged to almost any country. The eyebrows and cast-down lashes said that her eyes were dark, but the pure pale complexion, the delicate straight features, the thick brown hair might, under circumstances, have been claimed by any nation, although had I met her alone I should have said she was English. She was well but plainly dressed, and her manner told me she was no stranger to the church. She did not look from side to side, and up and down, after the way of a sightseer. She sat without moving until her companion had finished her prayers. So far as one could judge from her appearance she was in church for no particular object, neither devotional nor critical. Probably she may have come to bear the old woman at her side company. This old woman, who had the appearance of a superior kind of servant, seemed from the passionate appeals she was addressing to heaven to be in want of many things. I could see her thin lips working incessantly, and although her words were inaudible it was evident her petitions were heart-spoken and sincere.

But the girl by her side neither joined her in her prayers nor looked at her. Ever motionless as a statue—her eyes ever cast down—apparently wrapped in deep thought, and, I fancied, sad thought, she sat, showing us the while no more of her face than that perfect profile. Kenyon had certainly not over-praised her. Her's was a face which had a peculiar attractiveness for me, the utter repose of it not being the least of that charm. I was growing very anxious to see her full face, but as I could not do so without positive rudeness, was compelled to wait until she might chance to turn her head.

Presently the old Italian woman appeared to think she had done her religious duty. Seeing she was preparing to cross herself I rose and sauntered down the church toward the door. In a few minutes the girl and her companion passed me, and I was able to see her to better advantage, as she waited whilst the old woman dipped her fingers in the holy water. She was undoubtedly beautiful; but there was something strange in her beauty. I made this discovery when, for a moment, her eyes met mine. Dark and glorious as those eyes were there was a dreamy, far-away look in them—a look that seemed to pass over one and see what was behind the object gazed at. This look gave me a curious impression, but as it was only for a second that my eyes met hers, I could scarcely say whether the impression was a pleasant or an unpleasant one.

The girl and her attendant lingered a few moments at the door, so that Kenyon and I passed out before them. By common consent we paused outside. The action may have been a rude one, but we were both anxious to see the departure of the girl whose appearance had so greatly interested us. As we came through the door of the church I noticed a man standing near the steps—a middle-aged man of gentlemanly appearance. He was rather round-shouldered and wore spectacles. Had I felt any interest in determining his station in life I should have adjudged him to one of the learned professions. There could be no mistake as to his nationality; he was Italian to the backbone. He was evidently waiting for someone; and when the girl, followed by the old woman, came out of San Giovanni, he stepped forward and accosted them. The old woman gave a little sharp cry of surprise. She took his hand and kissed it. The girl stood apparently apathetic. It was evident that the gentleman's business lay with the old servant. He spoke a few words to her; then drawing her aside the two walked away to some distance, under the shadow of the church, and to all appearance were talking earnestly and volubly, but ever and anon casting a look in the direction of the girl.

As her companion left her she walked on a few paces, then paused and turned as though waiting for the old woman. Now it was that we were able to see her perfect figure and erect carriage to full advantage. Being some little way off, we could look at her without committing an act of rudeness or indiscretion.

'She is beautiful,' I said, more to myself than to Kenyon.

'Yes, she is—but not so beautiful as I thought. There is something wanting, yet it is impossible to say what it is. Is it animation or expression?'

'I can see nothing wanting,' I said, so enthusiastically that Kenyon laughed aloud.

'Do English gentlemen stare at their own countrywomen and appraise them in public places, like this; or is it a custom adopted for the benefit of Italians?'

This impudent question was asked by someone close to my side. We turned simultaneously, and saw a tall man of about thirty standing just behind us. His features were regular, but their effect was not a pleasant one. You felt at a glance that a sneering mouth was curtained by the heavy moustache, and that those dark eyes and eyebrows were apt to frown with sullen anger. At present the man's expression was that of haughty arrogance—a peculiarly galling expression, especially so I find when adopted by a foreigner toward an Englishman. That he was a foreigner it was easy to see, in spite of his perfectly accented English.

A hot reply was upon my lips, but Kenyon, who was a young man of infinite resource and well able to say and do the right thing in the right place, was before me. He raised his hat and made a sweeping bow, so exquisitely graduated that it was impossible to say where apology ended and mockery began.

'Signor,' he said, 'an Englishman travels through your fair land to see and praise all that is beautiful in nature and art. If our praise offends we apologize.'

The man scowled, hardly knowing whether my friend was in jest or in earnest.

'If we have done wrong will the Signor convey our apologies to the lady? His wife, or shall I say his daughter?'

As the man was young, the last question was sarcastic.

'She is neither,' he rapped out. Kenyon bowed.

'Ah, then a friend. Let me congratulate the Signor, and also congratulate him on his proficiency in our language.'

The man was growing puzzled; Kenyon spoke so pleasantly and naturally.

'I have spent many years in England,' he said, shortly.

'Many years! I should scarcely have thought so, the Signor has not picked up that English peculiarity which is far more important than accent or idiom.'

Kenyon paused and looked into the man's face so innocently and inquiringly that he fell into the trap.

'And pray what may that be?' he asked.

'To mind one's own business,' said Kenyon, shortly and sharply, turning his back to the last speaker, as if the discussion was at an end.

The tall man's face flushed with rage. I kept my eye upon him, fearing he would make an assault upon my friend, but he thought better of it. With a curse he turned on his heel, and the matter ended.

While this conversation was in progress, the old Italian woman had left her learned-looking friend, and having rejoined the young girl, the two went upon their way. Our ill-conditioned Italian, after his discomfiture, walked across to the man who had been talking to the old servant, and taking his arm went with him in another direction. They were soon out of sight.

Kenyon did not propose to follow the steps of the first couple, and I, even had I wished to do so, was ashamed to suggest such a thing. Still, I am afraid that a resolution as to visiting San Giovanni again tomorrow was forming in my mind.

But I saw her no more. How many times I went to that church I dare not say. Neither the fair girl nor her attendant crossed my path again whilst in Turin. We met our impertinent friend several times in the streets, and were honoured by a dark scowl which passed unnoticed; but of that sweet girl with the pale face and strange dark eyes we caught no glimpse.

It would be absurd to say I had fallen in love with a woman I had seen only for a few minutes—to whom I had never spoken—whose name and abode were unknown to me; but I must confess that, so far as looks went, I was more interested in this girl than in anyone I had ever seen. Beautiful as she was, I could scarcely say why I felt this attraction or fascination. I had met many, many beautiful women. Yet, for the slender chance of seeing this one again I lingered on in Turin until Kenyon—my good-tempered friend's patience was quite exhausted—declared that unless I quitted at once, he would go away alone. At last I gave in. Ten days had passed by without the chance encounter I was waiting for. We folded up our tents and started for fresh scenes.

From Turin we went southwards—to Genoa, Florence, Rome and Naples, and other minor places; then we went across to Sicily, and at Palermo, according to arrangement, were received on board a yacht belonging to another friend. We had taken our journey easily, staying as long as it suited us in each town we visited, so that by the time the yacht had finished her cruise and borne us back to England, the summer was nearly over.

Many and many a time since leaving Turin I had thought of the girl I had seen at San Giovanni—thought of her so often that I laughed at myself for my folly. Until now I had never carried in my mind for so long a period the remembrance of a woman's face. There must, for me, have been some-thing strangely bewitching in her style of beauty. I recalled every feature—I could, had I been an artist, have painted her portrait from memory. Laugh at my folly as I would, I could not conceal from myself that, short as time was during which I had seen her, the impression made upon me was growing stronger each day, instead of fainter. I blamed myself for leaving Turin before I had met her again—even if for that purpose it had been necessary to linger there for months. My feeling was that by quitting the place I had lost a chance which comes to a man but once in a lifetime.

Kenyon and I parted in London. He was going to Scotland after grouse, I had not yet quite settled my autumn plans, so I resolved to stay, at any rate for a few days, in town.

Was it chance or was it fate? The first morning after my arrival in London, business led me to Regent Street. I was walking slowly down the broad thoroughfare, but my thoughts were far away. I was trying to argue away an insane longing which was in my mind—a longing to return at once to Turin. I was thinking of the dim church and the fair young face I saw three months ago. Then, as in my mind's eye I saw that girl and her old attendant in church, I looked up and here, in the heart of London, they stood before me!

Amazed as I was, no thought of being mistaken entered my head. Unless it was a dream or an illusion, there came the one I had been thinking of so often, walking towards me, with the old woman at her side. They might have just stepped out of San Giovanni. There was a little change in the appearance of the old woman: she was dressed more like an English servant; but the girl was the same. Beautiful, more beautiful than ever, I thought as my heart gave a great leap. They passed me; I turned impulsively and followed them with my eyes.

Yes, it was Fate! Now I had found her in this unexpected manner I would take care not to lose sight of her again. I attempted to disguise my feelings no longer. The emotion which had thrilled me as I stood once more face to face with her told me the truth. I was in love—deeply in love. Twice, only twice, I had seen her, but that was enough to convince me that if my lot was ever linked with another's, it must be with this woman's, whose name, home, or country, I knew not.

There was only one thing I could now do. I must follow the two women. So, for the next hour or more wherever they went, at a respectful distance, I followed. I waited whilst they entered one or two shops, and when their walk was resumed discreetly dogged their steps. I kept so far in the rear that my pursuit was bound to be unnoticed and could cause no annoyance. They soon turned out of Regent Street and walked on until they came to one of those many rows of houses in Maida Vale. I marked the house they entered, and as I passed by it, a few minutes afterwards, saw in the front window the girl arranging a few flowers in a vase. It was evident I had ascertained her abode.

It was Fate! I was in love and could only act as my passion impelled me. I must find out all about this unknown. I must make her acquaintance and so obtain the right of looking into those strange but beautiful eyes. I must hear her speak. I laughed again at the absurdity of being in love with a woman whose voice I had never heard, whose native language was a matter of uncertainty. But then, love is full of absurdities. When once he gets the whip hand he drives us in strange ways.

I formed a bold resolve. I retraced my steps and walked up to the house. The door was opened by a tidy-looking servant. 'Have you any rooms to let?' I asked; having jumped at the conclusion that the unknown was only lodging at the house.

The servant replied in the affirmative, and upon my expressing a wish to see the vacant rooms I was shown a dining-room and bedroom on the ground floor.

Had these rooms been dungeons instead of airy, cheerful apartments—had they been empty and bare instead of comfortably furnished—had the rent been fifty pounds a week instead of the moderate sum asked, I should have engaged them. I was very easy to deal with. The landlady was summoned and the bargain struck at once. If that good person had known state of my mind she might have reaped a golden harvest of her ground floor apartments. As it was, the only thing she was exacting in was the matter of references. I named several, then I paid a month's rent in advance and received her permission, as I had just returned to England and wanted a home at once, to enter into possession that very evening.

'By the by,' I said carelessly, as I left the house to get my luggage, 'I forgot to ask if you have other lodgers—no children, I hope?'

'No, sir—only a lady and her servant. They are on the first floor—very quiet people.'

'Thank you,' I said. 'I dare say I shall be very, comfortable. You may expect me about seven o'clock.'

I had re-engaged my old rooms in Walpole Street before the meeting with my unknown had changed my plans. I went back there, and after packing up all I wanted, informed the people of the house that I was going to stay at a friend's for a few weeks. The rooms were to be kept for me all the same. At seven o'clock I was at Maida Vale and duly installed.

It was the hand of Fate had wrought this—who could doubt it? This morning I was almost on my way to Turin in search of my love. This evening I am beneath the same roof. As I sit here in my arm-chair and see all kinds of beautiful visions wreathed in the smoke curling from my cigar, I can scarcely believe that she is within a few feet of me—that I shall see her tomorrow—the next day—for ever and ever! Yes, I am hopelessly in love—I go to bed thinking I shall dream of her; but, probably owing to the strange quarters, my dreams are far less pleasant. All night long I dream of the blind man who walked into a strange house and heard such fearful sounds!

CHAPTER IV

NOT FOR LOVE OR MARRIAGE

A WEEK has passed by. I am more in love than ever. I am now satisfied as to the thoroughness of my passion; certain that this sudden love of mine will endure as long as my life, that it is no transient flush to fade away with time or absence. Whether my suit be successful or not this woman will be my first and last love.

As yet I have made little progress in the furthering of my desire. I see her every day, because I watch for her coming and going; and every time I see her I find fresh charms in her face and graces in her figure. Yet Kenyon was right. Hers is a peculiar style of beauty. That pale pure face, those dark dreamy far-away eyes, are out of the common run of woman-hood. It may be this accounts for the strange fascination she has for me. Her carriage is upright and graceful; she walks always at the same pace; her face is always grave, and it seems to me she seldom speaks to that old companion or servant who never quits her side. I am beginning to look upon her as a riddle, and wonder if the key will ever be mine.

I have found out some few things about her. Her name is Pauline—a sweet and suitable name—Pauline March. She is therefore English, although I sometimes hear her saying a few words in Italian to old Teresa, her servant. She seems to know no one, and, so far as I can learn, no one knows more about her than I do—I, at least, know she came from Turin, and that is more than my informants knew.

I still occupy my rooms, waiting my chance. It is tantalizing to live in the same house with the one you love and find no opportunity of even commencing the siege. That old Teresa guards her charge like a Spanish duenna. Her dark eyes glance quickly and suspiciously at me whenever I meet the two women, and bid them the good-morning or good-evening which a fellow-lodger may venture upon. As yet I have got no further than these cold civilities. Pauline's eyes and manner give me no encouragement. She acknowledges my salutation gravely, distantly, and apathetically. It is clear to me that love at first sight is not bound to be reciprocal. I comfort myself by thinking that Fate must have something in store for me, or Pauline and I would never have been brought face to face again.

So all I can do is to lurk behind the thick red curtains of my window and watch my love, guarded by that old cat Teresa, go out and come in. I am obliged now to exercise due caution in this proceeding, as the duenna once caught sight of me, and now each time they pass I see her fierce eyes peering into my hiding place. I am beginning to hate Teresa.

Yet if I have done little, I am in the same house, breathing the same air as Pauline, and I am a patient man and can wait for my opportunity. It will be sure to come at last.

This is how it came. One evening I heard a fall, a clatter of china and a cry of distress. I ran out of my room and found Teresa lying on the stairs amid the ruins of the landlady's best tea set, and groaning earnestly. My chance had come!

With the shameless hypocrisy of love, I ran to her aid, as eager to help her as though she had been my mother. I endeavoured, in the most tender manner, to raise her; but she sank back, wailing out something about 'one of ze foots broke'. It was clear that Teresa's English was not her strong point; so I asked her in Italian what was the matter. She brightened up as she heard her own language, and I found that she had sprained her knee so severely that she was unable to rise. I told her that I would carry her to her room, and without more ado picked her up and bore her upstairs.

Pauline was standing on the landing. Her large dark eyes were opened wide, her whole appearance that of affright. I paused a moment and explained what had happened, then I took the old woman into the room which she occupied and laid her on the bed. The servant of the house was sent for a doctor, and, as I retired, Pauline thanked me quietly, but I fancied listlessly, for my kindness. Those dreamy eyes met mine, yet scarcely seemed to know it. Yes, I was obliged to confess it, my goddess was in manner apathetic—but then, her beauty! Those refined regular features, the girlish but well-formed figure—the thick brown hair, even those strange dark eyes. Surely there was no woman in the world to compare with her!

She gave me her hand at parting—a small well-formed, soft hand. I could scarcely refrain from pressing my lips to it—I could scarcely refrain from telling her then and there that for months I had thought of her and her only—but injudicious as such proceedings might have been at a first meeting they would have been doubly so whilst old Teresa was lying, and, in spite of her pains, with suspicious eyes watching every movement of mine; so I could only express a wish to be of further service to her and bow myself out discreetly.

But the ice was broken—our hands had met. Pauline and I were strangers no longer!

Old Teresa's sprain, although not such a serious affair as she fancied, kept her indoors for several days. I hoped this would enable me to improve my acquaintance with her mistress, but the result was not commensurate with the hope. For the first few days Pauline, so far as I knew, did not leave the house. Once or twice I met her on the stairs and, assuming a fictitious interest in the old woman, kept her in conversation for a minute or two. It seemed to me that she was painfully shy—so shy that the conversation I would fain have prolonged, after a little while died a natural death. I was not conceited enough to attribute her shyness and reticence to the same cause which made me blush and stammer as I spoke to her.

At last, one morning I saw her leave the house alone. I took my hat and followed her. She was walking up and down the pavement in front of the house. I joined her, and, after the usual inquiry for Teresa, continued at her side. I must make an attempt to establish matters on a better footing between us.

'You have not been long in England, Miss March?' I said.

'Some time—some months,' she replied.

'I saw you in the spring at Turin—in church, at San Giovanni.' She raised her eyes and met mine with a strange, puzzled look.

'You were there with your old servant—one morning,' I continued.

'Yes—we often went there.'

'You are English, I suppose—your name is not an Italian one?'

'Yes, I am English.'

She spoke as though not quite certain about it—or as if it was a matter of complete indifference.

'Your home is here—You are not going back to Italy?'

'I don't know—I cannot tell.'

Pauline's manner was very unsatisfying. I made many attempts to learn something about her habits and tastes. Did she play or sing—was she fond of music, of pictures, of flowers, of the stage, of travelling? Had she many relations and friends? Directly and indirectly, I asked her all these questions.

Her replies were unsatisfactory. Either she evaded the questions, as if determined I should know nothing about her, or she did not seem to understand them. Many of them I felt sure puzzled her. At the end of our little promenade she remained as great a mystery to me as before. The only comfort I could take was that she displayed no wish to shun me. We passed and repassed the house several times, but she did not suggest re-entering, as she might have done had she wished to get rid of me. There was no trace of coquetry in her manner—quiet and reserved as I found her, she was at least simple and natural—and she was very beautiful, and I was very, very much in love!

It was not long before I discovered that old Teresa's black eyes were watching us from behind the blind of the drawing-room. She must have crept from her bed to see that her charge got into no mischief. I chafed at the espionage, but as yet it was too early to escape from it.

Before Teresa could hobble out of doors I had met Pauline more than once in the same way. She seemed, I was glad to believe, pleased when I joined her. The difficulty I laboured under was to make her talk. She would listen to all I had to say without comment and without reply, save yes or no. If, by a rare chance, she asked a question or spoke a longer sentence than usual, the effort was never sustained. I attributed a great deal of this to shyness and to her secluded life—for the only person she had to speak to was that terrible old Teresa.

Although every word and action of Pauline's told me she was well educated and well bred, I was certainly surprised at her ignorance of literature. If I quoted an author, mentioned a book by name, the remark passed unnoticed; or she looked at me as if puzzled by my allusion, or distressed at her own ignorance. Although I had now seen her several times, I was not satisfied at the progress I had made. I knew I had not as yet struck the key-note of her nature.

As soon as the old servant, duenna, friend, or what she was, grew well, I heard some startling news. My landlady asked me if I could recommend her apartments to any friend of mine—such another as myself, she was good enough to say—Miss March was going to leave, and the landlady thought she would prefer taking a gentleman in her place.

I felt certain this was a countermove of that old hag Teresa's. She had cast venomous glances at me when we passed each other on the stairs; had responded surlily when I asked if she had quite recovered from the effects of her accident—in a word, I knew she was my enemy; that she had discovered my feelings toward Pauline and was doing her best to keep us apart. I had no means of knowing the extent of her power or influence over the girl, but I had some time since ceased to regard her as anything more than a servant. The intelligence that my fellow-lodgers were about to quit showed me that to bring my love for Pauline to a successful issue, I must in some way make matters straight with this unpleasant old attendant.

That same evening, as I heard her coming down the stairs, I threw open my door and stood face to face with her.

'Signora Teresa,' I said, with high-flown politeness, 'will it please you to step into my room? I wish to speak to you.'

She gave me a quick, suspicious glance, but nevertheless complied with my request. I closed the door and placed a chair for her.

'Your poor knee—is it quite well?' I asked sympathetically, and in Italian.

'It is quite well, Signor,' she replied laconically.

'Will you take a glass of sweet wine? I have some here.'

Teresa, in spite of our inimical relations, made no objection, so I filled a glass and watched her sip it approvingly.

'Is the Signorina—Miss March well? I have not seen her today.'

'She is well.'

'It is about her I wish to speak to you—you have guessed that?'

'I have guessed it.' As she spoke Teresa gave me a sullen, defiant look.

'Yes,' I continued, 'your vigilant, faithful eyes have seen what I have no wish to conceal. I love the Signorina Pauline.'

'She is not to be loved,' said Teresa, sulkily.

'One so beautiful must be loved. I love her and will marry her.'

'She is not to be married.'

'Listen, Teresa. I say I will marry her. I am a gentleman and rich. I have 50,000 lire a year.'

The amount of my income, magnificent when reduced to her native coinage, was not without its expected effect. If her eyes, as they met mine, were as unfriendly as ever, their look of astonishment and increasing respect told me I was appealing to her tenderest feeling—cupidity.

'Now tell me why I should not marry the Signorina? Tell me who her friends are, that I may see them and ask her in marriage?'

'She is not for marriage.'

This was all I could get from the old woman. She would tell me nothing about Pauline's family or friends. She would only reiterate that she was not for love or for marriage.

I had but one chance left. Teresa's eager look when I mentioned the income I possessed had impressed me. I must condescend to the vulgar act of direct bribery; the end would justify the means.

As I was so often travelling it was my habit to carry a large sum of money on my person. I drew out my pocket-book and counted out a hundred pounds in new crisp notes. Teresa eyed them hungrily.

'You know what these are worth?' I said. She nodded. I pushed a couple of the notes toward her. Her skinny hand seemed twitching with the desire to grasp them.

'Tell me who Miss March's friends are and take these two notes; all the rest shall be yours on the day we are married.'

The old woman sat silent for a while, but I knew temptation was assailing her. Presently I heard her murmuring, '50,000 lire! 50,000 lire a year!' The spell worked. At last she rose.

'Are you going to take the money?' I asked.

'I cannot. I dare not. I am bound. But—'

'But what?'

'I will write. I will say what you say to il dottore.'

'Who is the doctor? I can write to him or see him.'

'Did I say il dottore? It was a slip. No, you must not write. I will ask him and he must decide.'

'You will write at once?'

'At once.' Teresa, with a lingering glance at the money, turned to leave me.

'You had better take these two notes, I said, handing them to her.

She buttoned them in the bosom of her dress with feverish delight.

'Tell me, Teresa,' I said, coaxingly, 'tell me if you think—if the Signorina—Pauline—cares at all for me?'

'Who knows?' answered the old woman, testily; 'I do not know—but again I say to you she is not for love or marriage.'

Not for love or marriage! I laughed aloud as I thought of the old woman's absurd and oft-repeated assertion. If on the earth there was one woman more than another made for love and marriage it was my beautiful Pauline! I wondered what Teresa could mean; then remembering the fervour with which she prayed in San Giovanni I decided that, being an ardent Roman Catholic, she wished Pauline to take the veil. This theory would explain everything.

Now that I had bought Teresa I looked forward to the enjoyment of Pauline's society without espionage or interruption. The old woman had taken my money, and no doubt would do her best to earn more. If I could persuade the girl to let me pass several hours of each day in her company I need fear no hindrance from Teresa. The bribe had been accepted, and, although I blushed at the expedient to which I had been compelled to resort, it had been successful.

I was obliged to defer any further attempt at lovemaking until the next evening, as an important piece of business had to be attended to in the morning. It kept me away from home for several hours, and when at last I returned to Maida Vale I was thunderstruck to hear that my fellow-lodgers had left the house. The landlady had no idea whither they had gone. Teresa, who it appears always acted as purse-bearer, had paid her dues and had departed with her young mistress. There was nothing more to tell.

I threw myself into my chair, cursing Italian guile; yet, as I thought of Italian cupidity, not altogether hopeless. Perhaps Teresa would write or come to me. I had not forgotten the eager looks she cast upon my money. But day after day passed without letter or message.

I spent those days, for the most part, wandering about the streets in the vain hope of encountering the fugitives. It was only after this second loss that I really knew the extent of my passion. I cannot describe the longing I had to see that fair face once more. Yet, I feared the love was all on my side. If Pauline had felt even a passing interest in me she could scarcely have left in this secret and mysterious manner. Her heart was yet to be won, and I knew that unless I won it no woman's love would to me be worth having.

I should have returned to my old lodgings in Walpole Street had it not been that I feared to quit Maida Vale, lest Teresa, if she should be faithful to her engagements, might miss me. So I lingered on there until ten days went slowly by; then, just as I was beginning to despair, a letter came.

It was written in a delicate pointed Italian style and signed Manuel Ceneri. It simply said that the writer would have the honour of calling upon me about noon today.

Nothing was hinted at as to the object of the visit, but I knew it could be connected with only one thing—the desire of my heart. Teresa, after all, had not played me false. Pauline would be mine. I waited with feverish impatience until this unknown Manuel Ceneri should make his appearance.

A few minutes after twelve he was announced and shown into my room. I recognized him at once. He was the middle-aged man with rather round shoulders who had talked to Teresa under the shade of San Giovanni at Turin. Doubtless he was 'il dottore' spoken of by the old woman as being the arbiter of Pauline's fate.

He bowed politely as he entered, cast one quick look at me as if trying to gather what he could from my personal appearance, then seated himself in the chair I offered him.

'I make no apology for calling,' he said; 'you will no doubt guess why I come.' His English was fluent, but the foreign accent very marked.

'I hope I guess correctly,' I replied.

'I am Manuel Ceneri. I am a doctor by profession. My sister was Miss March's mother. I have come from Geneva on your account.'

'Then you know what the wish—the great wish of my life is?'

'Yes, I know. You want to marry my niece. Now, Mr Vaughan, I have many reasons for wishing my niece to remain single, but your proposal has induced me to reconsider the matter.'

Pauline might have been a bale of cotton, so impassively did her uncle speak of her future.

'In the first place,' he went on, 'I am told you are well born and rich. Is that so?'

'My family is respectable. I am well connected and may be called rich.'

'You will satisfy me on the latter point, I suppose.'

I bowed stiffly, and taking a sheet of paper wrote a line to my solicitors, asking them to give the bearer the fullest information as to my resources. Ceneri folded up the note and placed it in his pocket. Perhaps I showed the annoyance I felt at the mercenary exactness of his inquiries.

'I am bound to be particular in this matter,' he said, 'as my niece has nothing.'

'I expect nothing or wish for nothing.'

'She had money once—a large fortune. It was lost long ago. You will not ask how or where?'

'I can only repeat my former words.'

'Very well—I feel I have no right to refuse your offer. Although she is half Italian, her manners and habits are English. An English husband will suit her best. You have not yet, I believe, spoken of love to her?'

'I have had no opportunity. I should no doubt have done so, but as soon as our acquaintance commenced she was taken away.'

'Yes, my instructions to Teresa were strict. It was only on condition she obeyed her that I allowed Pauline to live in England.'

Although this man spoke as one who had absolute authority over his niece, he had not said one word which evinced affection. So far as that went, she might have been a stranger to him.

'But now, I suppose,' I said, 'I shall be allowed to see her?'

'Yes—on conditions. The man who marries Pauline March must be content to take her as she is. He must ask no questions, seek to know nothing of her birth and family, nothing of her early days. He must be content to know that she is a lady, that she is very beautiful, and that he loves her. Will this suffice?'

The question was such a strange one that even in the height of my passion I hesitated.

'I will say this much,' added Ceneri, 'she is good and pure—her birth is equal to your own. She is an orphan and her only near relative is myself.'

'I am content,' I cried, holding out my hand to seal the compact. 'Give me Pauline, I ask no more.'

Why should I not be content? What did I want to know about her family, her antecedents, or her history? So madly did I long to call that beautiful girl mine that, I believe, had Ceneri told me she was worthless and disgraced among women, I should have said, 'Give her to me and let her begin life anew as my wife.' Men do such things for love!

'Now, Mr Vaughan,' said the Italian, drawing his hand from mine; 'my next question will astonish you. You love Pauline, and I believe she is not indifferent to you—'

He paused and my heart beat at the thought. 'Will your arrangements permit of an early marriage—an immediate marriage? Can I upon my return to the Continent in a few days leave her future in your hands entirely?'

'I would marry her today if it were possible,' I cried.

'We need not be so impetuous as that—but could you arrange for, say, the day after tomorrow?'

I stared at him—I could scarcely believe I heard correctly. To be married to Pauline within a few hours! There must be something in the background of such bliss! Ceneri must be a madman! Yet, even from the hands of a madman how could I refuse my happiness?

'But I don't know if she loves me—would she consent?' I stammered,

'Pauline is obedient and will do as I wish. You can woo her after her marriage instead of before it.'

'But can it be done on so short a notice?'

'I believe there are such things as special licences to be bought. You are wondering at my suggestion. I am bound to return to Italy almost at once. Now, I put it to you—can I, in the present circumstances, leave Pauline here with only a servant to look after her? No, Mr Vaughan, strange as it may seem, I must either see her your wife before I leave or I must take her back with me. The latter may be unfortunate for you, as here I have only myself to consider, whilst abroad there may be others to consult, and perhaps I must change my mind.'

'Let us go to Pauline and ask her,' I said, rising impatiently.

'Certainly,' said Ceneri, gravely, 'we will go at once.'

Till now I had been sitting with my back to the window. As I faced the light I noticed the Italian doctor look very straight at me.

'Your face seems quite familiar to me, Mr Vaughan, although I cannot recall where I have seen you.'

I told him he must have seen me outside San Giovanni while he was talking to old Teresa. He remembered the occurrence and appeared satisfied. Then we called a cab and drove to Pauline's new abode.

It was not so very far away. I wondered I had not encountered either Pauline or Teresa in my rambles. Perhaps they had both kept to the house to avoid the meeting.

'Would you mind waiting in the hall a minute?' asked Ceneri as we entered the house. 'I will go and prepare Pauline for your coming.'

I would have waited a month in a dungeon for the reward in prospect; so I sat down on the polished mahogany chair and wondered if I was in my right senses.

Presently old Teresa came to me. She looked scarcely more amiable than before.

'Have I done well?' she whispered in Italian.

'You have done well—I will not forget.'

'You will pay me and blame me for nothing. But listen— once more I say it—the Signorina is not for love or marriage.'

Superstitious old fool! Were Pauline's charms to be buried in a nunnery?

Then a bell rang and Teresa left me. In a few minutes she reappeared and conducted me upstairs to a room in which I found my beautiful Pauline and her uncle. She raised her dark dreamy eyes and looked at me—the most infatuated man could not have flattered himself that the light of love was in them.

I fully expected that Doctor Ceneri would have left us to arrange matters alone; but no—he took me by the hand and in a stately manner led me to his niece.

'Pauline, you know this gentleman.'

She bowed. 'Yes, I know him.'

'Mr Vaughan,' continued Ceneri, 'does us the honour of asking you to be his wife.'

I could not permit all my wooing to be done by proxy, so I stepped forward and took her hand in mine.

'Pauline,' I whispered, 'I love you—since first I saw you I have loved you—will you be my wife?'

'Yes, if you wish it,' she replied softly, but without even changing colour.

'You cannot love me now, but you will by and by—will you not, my darling?'

She did not respond to my appeal, but then she did not repulse me, neither did she strive to withdraw her hand from mine; she remained calm and undemonstrative as ever; but I threw my arm round her, and, in spite of Ceneri's presence, kissed her passionately. It was only when my lips touched her own that I saw the colour rise to her cheek and knew that she was moved.

She disengaged herself from my embrace, glanced at her uncle, who stood impassive as if he had witnessed nothing out of the common, and then she fled from the room.

'I think you had better go now,' said Ceneri. 'I will arrange everything with Pauline. You must do on your part all that is necessary for the day after tomorrow.'

'It is very sudden,' I said.

'It is, but it must be so—I cannot wait an hour longer. You had better leave me now and return tomorrow.'

I went away with my head in a whirl—I was uncertain what to do. The temptation to call Pauline my own in so short a time was great; but I could not deceive myself by thinking that she cared for me at all, as yet. But, as Ceneri said, I could do my wooing after marriage. Still I hesitated. The hurried proceeding was so strange. Ardently as I desired to wed Pauline I wished I could have first won her. Would it not be better to let her uncle take her to Italy, then to follow her and learn if she could love me? Against this prudent course came Ceneri's vague threat, that in such an event his mind might be changed—and more than all, I was desperately in love. Although it could only be for her beauty that I loved her, I was madly in love. Fate had thrown us together. She had escaped me twice—now the third time she was offered to me unreservedly. I was superstitious enough to think that if I rejected or postponed accepting the gift, it would be withdrawn forever. No—come what will, in two days' time Pauline shall be my wife!

I saw her the next day, but never alone. Ceneri was with us all the time. Pauline was sweet, silent, shy and languid. I had much to do—much to see to. Never was a wooing so short or so strange as mine. By the evening all arrangements were made, and by ten o'clock the next morning Gilbert Vaughan and Pauline March were man and wife—those two who had not in their lifetime even conversed for a time amounting, say, to three hours, were linked together for better or worse till death should part them!

Ceneri left immediately the ceremony was over, and, to my astonishment, Teresa announced her intention of accompanying him. She did not fail to wait on me for the promised reward, which I gave her freely and fully. My heart's desire was to wed Pauline, and by her aid it had been compassed.

Then, with my beautiful bride, I started for the Scottish lochs, to begin the wooing which should have been completed before the final step had been taken.

CHAPTER V

BY LAW, NOT LOVE

PROUD and happy as I felt when seated side by side with Pauline in the railway carriage which was taking us to the north; fortunate as I told myself I was to have won such a fair bride; great as my love was for the sweet girl who had just vowed herself mine forever, Ceneri's extraordinary stipulation kept recurring to my mind—the man who marries Pauline March must be content to take her as she is; to wish to know nothing of her past.

Not for one moment did I think such a contract could be enforced. As soon as I had succeeded in making Pauline love me, she would surely wish to tell me all her history—there would be no need to ask for it—the confidence would then be given as a matter of course. When she had learned the secret of love, all other secrets would cease between us.

My wife looked very beautiful as she sat with her head leaning against the dark cloth of the carriage. Her clear-cut refined features showed in that position advantageously. Her face, as usual, was pale and calm; her eyes were cast down. A woman to be indeed proud of, to worship, to cherish, and—how sweet it seemed to whisper the word to myself—my wife!

Yet I suspect none would have taken us for a newly married couple. At any rate there were no nudgings and sly glances among our fellow passengers. The ceremony had been so hurried on that no attempt had been made to invest Pauline with the usual bridal accessories. Her dress, although becoming and fashionable, was the one in which I had seen her several times. Neither of us had any brand new belongings to stamp us as being bound for a honeymoon; so the

54

only notice we attracted was the notice which was due to my wife's great and uncommon beauty.

The carriage was nearly full when we started from London, and as the strangeness of our new relations prevented our conversing in an ordinary way, by mutual consent we were all but silent; a few soft words in Italian were all I could trust myself to speak until we were alone.

At the first important station, the first place at which the train stopped for any time worth mentioning, I exercised a little diplomatic bribery, and changing our carriage we were installed in a compartment, the windows of which bore the magic word 'engaged'. Pauline and I were alone. I took her hand in mine.

'My wife!' I said, passionately, 'mine, only mine, for ever!'

Her hand lay listless and unresisting in my own. I pressed my lips to her cheek. She shrank not from my kiss, neither did she return it—she simply suffered it.

'Pauline!' I whispered, 'say once, "Gilbert, my husband".'

She repeated the words like a child learning a new lesson. My heart sank as her emotionless accents fell on my ears. I had a hard task before me!

I could not blame her. Why should she love me yet? Me, whose Christian name, I think, she heard yesterday for the first time? Better, far better, indifference than simulated love. She had become my wife simply because her uncle wished it. I could at least comfort myself by thinking the marriage had not been forced upon her; also that, so far as I could see, she entertained no dislike to me. I did not for one moment despair. I must now woo her humbly and reverently, as every man should woo his love. Certainly, as her husband, I did not stand in a worse position than when I was her fellow lodger and old Teresa was following my every movement with her black suspicious eyes.

I would win her, but until I could claim the rights which love would give, I resolved to take none of those with which the law had invested me. None save this, and this only once:

'Pauline,' I said, 'will you kiss me? Only once I ask it. It will make me happier; but if you would rather wait until we are better acquainted, I shall not complain.'

She leaned forward and kissed my forehead. Her young lips were red and warm, but they chilled me—in that kiss there was not a suspicion of the passion which was thrilling me.

I drew my hand from hers, and, still sitting beside her, began to do my best to make myself agreeable to the woman I loved. If I felt distressed and somewhat disappointed, I concealed it and strove to talk pleasantly and naturally—tried to ascertain what manner of woman I had married—to get at her likes and dislikes—to study her disposition—to determine her tastes—learn her wishes—read her thoughts, and eventually to make her regard me as one who would spend his life in rendering her happy.

When was it the idea first struck me—the horrible idea that even the peculiarity and novelty of situation could not altogether account for Pauline's apathy and lack of animation—that shyness alone could not be entirely responsible for the difficulty I experienced in making her talk to me, even in inducing her to answer my questions? I made every excuse for her. She was tired; she was upset; she could think of nothing else save the rash and sudden step taken today—more rash for her than for me—as I, at least, knew that I loved her. At last I, too, sank into silence, and miles and hours went by, whilst the bride and bridegroom sat side by side without exchanging a word, much less a caress. It was a strange situation—a strange journey!

And on and on the train rushed northwards—on and on until the dusk began to creep over the flying country; and I sat and looked at the listless but beautiful girl at my side, and wondered what our future life would be; but I did not despair, although the rattle of the train as it whirred along seemed to resolve itself into a dreamy rhythm, and reiterated without ceasing old Teresa's sullen words, 'She is not for love or marriage—not for love or marriage.'

Darker and darker it grew outside, and as the carriage light fell on the pure, white face of the girl beside me; as I watched its never changing expression; its beautiful but never varying pallor, a strange fear came over me—a fear lest she was wrapped in an armour of ice which no love would ever thaw. Then tired, weary and almost dispirited I sank into a kind of sleep. The last thing I could remember before my eyes closed was that, in spite of my resolution, I took that white, well-shaped, unresisting hand in my own, and slept still holding it.

Sleep! Yes, it was sleep, if sleep means anything but rest and peace. Never, since the night I heard it, had that woman's stifled moaning come back to me so clearly; never had my dreams so nearly approached the reality of the terror which the blind man had felt years ago. Right thankful I was when the haunting cry rose shriller and shriller, and, at last, culminated by resolving itself into the shrieking whistle, which told me we were near to Edinburgh. I loosed my wife's hand and recalled my senses. That dream must have been a vivid one, for it left me with the beads of perspiration clammy on my brow.

Never having been to Edinburgh, and wishing to see something of the city, I had proposed staying there for two or three days. During the journey I had suggested this to my wife. She had agreed to it as though place or time was a matter of little moment to her. Nothing, it seemed to me, awoke her interest!

We drove to the hotel and supped together. From our manner we might, at the most, have been friends, our intercourse for the time being confined to the usual civilities shown by a gentleman towards a lady in whose society he is thrown. Pauline thanked me for any little attention to her comfort, and that was all. The journey had been a long and trying one—she looked wearied out.

'You are tired, Pauline,' I said; 'would you like to go to your room?'

'I am very tired.' She spoke almost plaintively.

'Good night, then,' I said; 'tomorrow you will feel better, and we will look at the lions of the place.'

She rose, we shook hands and said good night. Pauline retired to her apartment while I went out for a ramble through the gas-lighted streets, and with a sad heart recalled the events of the day.

Husband and wife! The bitter mockery of the words! For in everything except the legal bond Pauline and I were as far apart as we were on that day when first I saw her at Turin. Yet this morning we had vowed to love and cherish each other until death did us part. Why had I been rash enough to take Ceneri at his word? Why not have waited until I had ascertained that the girl could love me, or at least ascertained that she had the power of loving at all? The apathy and utter indifference she displayed fell like a chill upon my heart. I had done a foolish thing—a thing that could never be undone. I must bear the consequences. Still I would hope—hope, particularly, for what tomorrow might bring forth.

I walked about for a long time, thinking over my strange position. Then I returned to the hotel and sought my own apartment. It was one of the suite of rooms I had engaged, and next to my wife's. I dismissed, as well as I could, all hopes and fears until the morning came, and, tired with the day's events, at last slept.

My bride and I did not visit the lochs as I had planned. In two days' time I had learned the whole truth—learned all I could know—all that I might ever know about Pauline. The meaning of the old woman's repeated phrase, 'she is not for love or marriage,' was manifested to me. The reason why Dr Ceneri had stipulated that Pauline's husband should be content to take her without inquiring into her early life was clear. Pauline—my wife—my love, had no past!

Or no knowledge of the past. Slowly at first, then with swift steps, the truth came home to me. Now I knew how to account for that puzzled, strange look in those beautiful eyes—knew the reason for the indifference, the apathy she displayed. The face of the woman I had married was fair as the morn; her figure was perfect as that of a Grecian statue; her voice low and sweet; but the one thing which animates every charm—the mind—was missing!

How shall I describe her? Madness means something quite different from her state. Imbecility still less convey my meaning. There is no word I can find which is fitting to use. There was simply something missing from her intellect—as much missing as a limb may be from a body. Memory, except for comparatively recent events, she seemed to have none. The power of reasoning, weighing and drawing deductions seemed beyond her grasp. She appeared unable to recognize the importance or bearing of occurrences taking place around her. Sorrow and delight were emotions she was incapable of feeling. Nothing appeared to move her. Unless her attention was called to them she noticed neither persons nor places. She lived as by instinct—rose, ate, drank, and lay down to rest as one not knowing why she did so. Such questions or remarks as came within the limited range of her capacity she replied to—those outside it passed unheeded, or else the shy troubled eyes sought for a moment the questioner's face, and left him as mystified as I had been when first I noticed that curious inquiring look.

Yet she was not mad. A person might have met her out in company, and after spending hours in her society might have carried away no worse impression than that she was shy and reticent. Whenever she did speak her words were as those of a perfectly sane woman; but as a rule her voice was only heard when the ordinary necessities of life demanded, or in reply to some simple question. Perhaps I should not be far wrong in comparing her mind to that of a child—but, alas! it was a child's mind in a woman's body—and that woman was my wife!

Life to her, so far as I could see, held neither mental pleasure nor pain. Considered physically, I found that she was more influenced by heat and cold than by any other agents. The sun would tempt her out of doors, or the cold wind would drive her in. She was by no means unhappy. She seemed quite content to sit by my side, or to walk and drive with me for hours without speaking. Her whole existence was a negative one.

And she was sweet and docile. She followed every suggestion of mine, fell in with every plan, was ready to go here, there, or everywhere, as I wished; but her compliance and obedience were as those of a slave to a new master. It seemed to me that all her life she must have been accustomed to obey someone. It was this habit which had so misled me—had almost made me think that Pauline loved me, or she would not have consented to that hasty marriage. Now, I knew that her ready obedience to her uncle's command was really due to the inability of her mind to offer resistance, and its powerlessness to comprehend the true meaning of the step she was taking.

Such was Pauline, my wife! A woman in her beauty and grace of person; a child in her clouded and unformed or stunted mind! And I, her husband, a strong man craving for love, might win from her, perchance, at last, what might be compared to the affection of a child to its parents, or a dog to its master.

As the truth, the whole truth, came home to me, I am not ashamed to say that I lay down and wept in bitter grief.

I loved her even now I knew all! I would not even have undone the marriage. She was my wife—the only woman I had ever cared for. I would fulfil my vow—would love her and cherish her. Her life, at least, should be as happy as my care could make it. But all the same I vowed I would have a fitting reckoning with that glib Italian doctor.

Him, I felt it was necessary I should see at once. From him I would wring all particulars. I would learn if Pauline had always been the same—if there was any hope that time and patient treatment would work an improvement. I would learn, moreover, the object of his concealment. I would, I swore, drag the truth from him, or it should cost me dear. Until I stood face to face with Ceneri I should find no peace.

I told Pauline it was necessary we should return to London immediately. She betrayed no surprise; raised no objections. She made her preparations at once, and was ready to accompany me when I willed it. This was another thing about her which puzzled me. So far as things mechanically went, she was as other people. In her toilet, even in her preparations for a journey, she needed no assistance. All her actions were those of a perfectly sane person; it was only when the mind was called upon to show itself that the deficiency became at all apparent.

It was grey morning when we reached Euston Station. We had travelled all night. I smiled bitterly as I stepped on to the platform; smiled at the contrast between my thoughts of today and those of a few mornings ago when I handed the wife I had so strangely won into the train, and told myself, as I followed her, that a life of perfect happiness was now about to begin.

And yet how fair the girl looked as she stood by my side on that wide platform! How strangely that air of repose, that sweet refined calm face, that general appearance of indifference, contrasted with the busy scene around us, as the train disgorged its contents. Oh, that I could sweep the clouds from her mind and make her what I wished!

I had found some difficulty in settling what course to pursue. I decided, after ventilating various schemes, that I would take Pauline to my own rooms in Walpole Street. I knew the people of the house well, and felt certain she would be taken care of during my absence; for, after a few hours' repose, it was my intention to start in search of Ceneri. I had written from Edinburgh to Walpole Street, telling the good people there to be ready for me and whom to expect; moreover, I had again appealed to my faithful old servant, Priscilla, and begged her to be at the house awaiting my arrival. For my sake, I knew she would show every kindness to my poor girl. So to Walpole Street we went.

All was in readiness for us. Priscilla received us with eyes full of curious wonder. I saw that her sympathies were at once enlisted by Pauline's appearance. After a cup of tea and something to eat, I begged Priscilla to lead my wife to her room, that she might take the rest she needed. Pauline, in her childlike, docile way, rose and followed the old woman.

'When you have seen to Mrs Vaughan's comforts, come back to me,' I said. 'I want to speak to you.'

Priscilla, no doubt, was only too eager to return to me. I felt she was brimming over with questions about my unexpected marriage; but I checked her volubility. My face must have told her that I had nothing pleasant to communicate. She sat down, and, as I desired her to do, listened without comment to my tale.

I was compelled to confide in someone. The old woman, I knew, was trustworthy and would keep my affairs secret. So I told her all, or nearly all. I explained as well as I could Pauline's peculiar mental state. I suggested all that my short experience brought to my mind, and I prayed Priscilla, by the love she bore me, to guard and be kind in my absence to the wife I loved. The promise being given I threw myself upon the sofa and slept for several hours.

In the afternoon I saw Pauline again. I asked her if she knew where I could write to Ceneri. She shook her head.

'Try and think, my dear,' I said.

She pressed her delicate finger tips against her brow. I had always noticed that trying to think always troubled her greatly.

'Teresa knew,' I said to assist her.

'Yes, ask her.'

'But she has left us, Pauline. Can you tell us where she is?'

Once more she shook her head hopelessly.

'He told me he lived in Geneva,' I said. 'Do you know the street?'

She turned her puzzled eyes to mine. I sighed, as I knew my questions were useless.

Still, find him I must. I would go to Geneva. If the man was a doctor, as he represented himself, he must be known there. If I could not find any trace of him at Geneva I would try Turin. I took my wife's hand.

'I am going away for a few days, Pauline. You will stay here until I return. Everyone will be kind to you. Priscilla will get you all you want.'

'Yes, Gilbert,' she said softly. I had taught her to call me Gilbert.

Then, after some last instructions to Priscilla, I started on my journey. As my cab drove from the door I glanced up at the window of the room in which I had left Pauline. She was standing there looking at me, and a great wave of joy came over my heart, for I fancied that her eyes were looking sad, like the eyes of one taking leave of a dear friend. It may have been only fancy, but, as I had never before even fancied the expression there, that look in Pauline's eyes was some comfort to carry away with me.

And now for Geneva and il dottore Ceneri!

CHAPTER VI

UNSATISFACTORY ANSWERS

I TRAVELLED in hot haste, as fast as steam would bear me, to Geneva; where I at once began my inquiries as to the whereabouts of Doctor Ceneri. I had hoped that finding him would be an easy matter. His words had given me the impression that he practised in the town. If so, many people must know him. But he had misled me or I had deceived myself. For several days I hunted high and low; inquired everywhere; but not a soul could I find who knew the man. I called on every doctor in the place; one and all professed entire ignorance of such a colleague. At last I felt certain that the name he had given me was a fictitious one, or that Geneva was not his abode. However obscure a doctor may be, he is sure to he known by some of his professional brethren in the same town. I decided to go to Turin and try my luck there.

It was on the eve of my intended departure. I was strolling about, feeling very sad at heart, and trying to persuade myself that I should fare better in Turin, when I noticed a man lounging along the opposite side of the street. As his face and bearing seemed familiar to me, I crossed the road to see him to better advantage. Being clothed in the inevitable tourist suit, he presented the appearance of an ordinary British traveller—so much so that I believed I must be mistaken. But I was right, after all. In spite of his changed attire, I recognized him the moment I drew near. He was the man with whom Kenyon had engaged in a wordy war outside San Giovanni— the man who had remonstrated with us for our expressed admiration of Pauline—the man who had walked away arm in arm with Ceneri.

The chance was too good a one to be lost. He would, at least, know where the doctor was to be found. I trusted his memory for faces was not so retentive as mine; that he would not connect me with the unpleasant passage which occurred when we last met. I walked up to him, and raising my hat requested him to favour me with a few moments' conversation.

I spoke in English. He gave me a quick, penetrating glance, then acknowledging my salutation, professed, in the same language, his wish to place himself at my service.

'I am trying to ascertain the address of a gentleman who I believe lives here. I think you will be able to assist me.'

He laughed. 'I will if I can—but being like yourself an Englishman, and knowing very few people, I fear I can be of little help to you.'

'I am anxious to find a doctor named Ceneri.'

The start he gave as he heard my words; the look, almost of apprehension, he cast on me, showed me that he recognized the name. But in a second he recovered himself.

'I cannot remember the name. I am sorry to say I am unable to help you.'

'But,' I said, in Italian, 'I have seen you in his company.'

He scowled viciously. 'I know no man of the name. Good morning.'

He raised his hat and strode away.

I was not going to lose him like that. I quickened my pace and came up with him.

'I must beg of you to tell me where I can find him. I must see him upon an important matter. It is no use denying that he is a friend of yours.'

He hesitated, then halted. 'You are strangely importunate, sir. Perhaps you will tell me your reason for your statement that the man you seek is my friend?'

'I saw you arm in arm with him.'

'Where, may I ask?'

'In Turin—last spring. Outside San Giovanni.'

He looked at me attentively. 'Yes, I remember your face now. You are one of those young men who insulted a lady, and whom I swore to chastise.'

'No insult was meant, but even had it been so, it might be passed over now.'

'No insult! I have killed a man for less than your friend said to me!'

'Please remember I said nothing. But that matters little. It is on behalf of his niece, Pauline, that I wish to see Dr Ceneri.'

A look of utter astonishment spread over his face. 'What have you to do with his niece?' he asked roughly.

'That is his business and mine. Now tell me where I can find him.'

'What is your name?' he asked curtly

'Gilbert Vaughan.'

'What are you?'

'An English gentleman—nothing more.'

He remained thoughtful for a few seconds. 'I can take you to Ceneri,' he said, 'but first I must know what you want with him, and why you mention Pauline's name? The street is not the place to talk in—let us go elsewhere.'

I led him to my hotel, to a room where we could talk at our ease.

'Now, Mr Vaughan,' he said, 'answer my question, and I may see my way to helping you. What has Pauline March to do with the matter?'

'She is my wife—that is all.'

He sprang to his feet—a fierce Italian oath hissed from his lips. His face was white with rage.

'Your wife!' he shouted. 'You lie—I say you lie!'

I rose, furious as himself, but more collected.

'I told you, sir, that I am an English gentleman. Either you will apologize for your words or I will kick you out of the room.'

He struggled with his passion and curbed it. 'I apologize,' he said, 'I was wrong. Does Ceneri know it?' he asked sharply.

'Certainly; he was present when we were married.'

His passion once more seemed upon the point of mastering him. '*Traditore!*' I heard him whisper fiercely to himself. '*Ingannatore!*' Then he turned to me with composed features.

'If so, I have nothing more to do save to congratulate you, Mr Vaughan. Your fortune is indeed enviable. Your wife is beautiful, and of course good. You will find her a charming companion.'

I would have given much to know why the mention of my marriage should have sent him into such a storm of rage, but I would have given more to have been able to fulfil my threat of kicking him out. The intonation of his last words told me that Pauline's state of mind was well known to him. I could scarcely keep my hands off the fellow; but I was compelled to restrain my anger, as without his aid I could not find Ceneri.

'Thank you,' I said quietly, 'now perhaps you will give me the information I want.'

'You are not a very devoted bridegroom, Mr Vaughan,' said the fellow mockingly. 'If Ceneri was at your wedding it could only have occurred a few days ago. It must be important business which tears you from the side of your bride.'

'It is important business.'

'Then I fear it must wait a few days. Ceneri is not in Geneva. But I have reason to think he may be here in about a week's time. I shall see him, and tell him you are here.'

'Let me know where to find him and I will call upon him. I must speak with him.'

'I imagine that will be as the doctor chooses. I can only make known your wishes to him.'

He bowed and left me. I felt that even now it was doubtful whether I should succeed in obtaining the interview with the mysterious doctor. It depended entirely whether he chose to grant it. He might come to Geneva and go away again without my being any the wiser, unless his friend or himself sent me some communication.

I idled away a week, and then began to fear that Ceneri had made up his mind to keep out of my way. But it was not so. A letter came one morning. It contained a few words only. 'You wish to see me. A carriage will call for you at eleven o'clock. M.C.'

At eleven o'clock an ordinary hired conveyance drove up to the hotel. The driver inquired for Mr Vaughan. I stepped in without a word, and was driven to a small house outside the town. Upon being shown into a room I found the doctor seated at a table covered with newspapers and letters. He rose, and shaking my hand begged me to be seated.

'You have come to Geneva to see me, I hear, Mr Vaughan?'

'Yes. I wished to ask you some questions respecting my wife.'

'I will answer all I can—but there are many to which I shall doubtless refuse to reply. You remember my stipulation?'

'Yes, but why did you not make me aware of my wife's peculiar mental state?'

'You had seen her yourself several times. Her state was the same as when she first proved so attractive to you. I am sorry you should think yourself deceived.'

'Why not have told me everything? Then I could have blamed no one.'

'I had so many reasons, Mr Vaughan. Pauline was a great responsibility on my shoulders. A great expense, for I am a poor man. And, after all, is the matter so very bad? She is beautiful, good, and amiable. She will make you a loving wife.'

'You wished to get rid of her, in fact.'

'Scarcely that altogether. There are circumstances—I cannot explain them—which made me glad to marry her to an Englishman of good position.'

'Without thinking what that man's feelings might be on finding the woman he loved little better than a child.'

I felt indignant, and showed my feelings very plainly. Ceneri took little notice of my warmth. He remained perfectly calm.

'There is another point to be considered. Pauline's case is, in my opinion, far from being hopeless. Indeed, I have always looked upon marriage as greatly adding to the chance of her recovery. If her mind to a certain extent is wanting, I believe that, little by little, it may be built up again. Or it may return as suddenly as it left her.'

My heart leapt at his words of hope. Cruelly as I felt I had been treated, tool that I had been made for this man's selfish ends, I was willing to accept the situation cheerfully if I had any hope held out to me.

'Will you give me all the particulars of my poor wife's state? I conclude she has not been always like this?'

'Certainly not. Her case is most peculiar. Some years ago she received a great shock—sustained a sudden loss. The effect was to entirely blot out the past from her mind. She rose from her bed after some weeks' illness with her memory a complete blank. Places were forgotten—friends were strangers to her. Her mind might, as you say, have been the mind of a child. But a child's mind grows, and, if treated properly, so will hers.'

'What was the cause of her illness—what shock?'

'That is one of the questions I cannot answer.'

'But I have a right to know.'

'You have a right to ask, and I have a right to refuse to speak.'

'Tell me of her family—her relatives.'

'She has none, I believe, save myself.'

I asked other questions, but could get no answers worth recording. I should return to England not much wiser than I left it. But there was one question to which I insisted on having a clear reply.

'What has that friend of yours—that English-speaking Italian, to do with Pauline?'

Ceneri shrugged his shoulders and smiled.

'Macari? I am glad to be able to answer something fully, Mr Vaughan. For a year or two before Pauline was taken ill,

Macari supposed himself to be in love with her. He is now furious with me for allowing her to get married. He declares he was only awaiting her recovery to try his own luck.'

'Why should he not have served your purpose as well as I seem to have?'

Ceneri looked at me sharply. 'Do you regret, Mr Vaughan?'

'No—not if there is a chance, even a slight chance. But I tell you, Dr Ceneri, you have deceived me shamefully.'

I rose to take my leave. Then Ceneri spoke with more feeling than he had as yet displayed.

'Mr Vaughan, do not judge me too harshly. I have wronged you, I admit. There are things you know nothing of. I must tell you more than I intended. The temptation to place Pauline in a position of wealth and comfort was irresistible. I am her debtor for a vast amount. At one time her fortune was about fifty thousand pounds. The whole of that I spent—'

'And dare to boast of it!' I said, bitterly.

He waved his hand with dignity.

'Yes. I dare to speak of it. I spent it all for freedom—for Italy. It was in my keeping as trustee. I, who would have robbed my own father, my own son, should I hesitate to take her money for such an end? Every farthing went to the great cause, and was well spent.'

'It was the act of a criminal to rob an orphan.'

'Call it what you like. Money had to be found. Why should I not sacrifice my honour for my country as freely as I would have sacrificed my life?'

'It is no use discussing it—the matter is ended.'

'Yes, but I tell you to show you why I wished to gain Pauline a home. Moreover, Mr Vaughan'—here his voice dropped to a whisper—'I was anxious to provide that home at once. I am bound on a journey—a journey of which I cannot see the end, much less the returning. I doubt whether I should have decided to see you had it not been for this. But the chances are we shall never meet again.'

'You mean you are engaged in some plot or conspiracy?'

'I mean what I have said—no more, no less. I will now bid you adieu.'

Angry as I was with the man, I could not refuse the hand he stretched out to me.

'Farewell,' he said, 'it may be that in some year or two I shall write to you and ask you if my predictions as to Pauline's recovery have been fulfilled; but do not trouble to seek me or to inquire for me if I am silent.'

So we parted. The carriage was waiting to take me back to the hotel. On my way thither I passed the man whom Ceneri had called Macari. He signalled to the driver to stop, and then entering the carriage sat beside me.

'You have seen the doctor, Mr Vaughan?' he asked.

'Yes. I have just come from him.'

'And have learned all you wish to know, I hope?'

'A great many of my questions have been answered.'

'But not all. Ceneri would not answer all.'

He laughed, and his laugh was cynical and mocking. I kept silence.

'Had you questioned me,' he continued, 'I might have told you more than Ceneri.'

'I came here to ask Dr Ceneri for all the information he could give me respecting my wife's mental state, of which I believe you are aware. If you can say anything that may be of use to me, I will beg you to speak.'

'You asked him what caused it?'

'I did. He told me a shock.'

'You asked him what shock. That he did not tell you?'

'He had his reasons for declining, I suppose.'

'Yes. Excellent reasons—family reasons.'

'If you can enlighten me, kindly do so.'

'Not here, Mr Vaughan. The doctor and I are friends. You might fly back and assault him, and I should get blamed. You are going back to England, I suppose?'

'Yes. I start at once.'

'Give me your address, and perhaps I will write; or, better still, if I feel inclined to be communicative, I will call upon you when I am next in London, and pay my respects to Mrs Vaughan at the same time.'

So eager was I to get at the bottom of the affair that I gave him my card. He then stopped the carriage and stepped out. He raised his hat, and there was a malicious triumph in his eyes as they met mine.

'Goodbye, Mr Vaughan. Perhaps after all you are to be congratulated upon being married to a woman whose past it is impossible to rake up.'

With this parting shaft—a shaft which struck deep and rankled—he left me. It was well he did so, before I caught him by the throat and strove to force him to explain his last words.

Longing to see my poor wife again, I went back to England with all speed.

CHAPTER VII

CLAIMING RELATIONSHIP

YES, she was glad to see me back! In her uncertain, clouded way she welcomed me. My great fear, that in the short time she would have entirely forgotten me, was groundless She knew me and welcomed me. My poor Pauline! If I could but find the way to bring those truant senses back once more!

For months and months nothing of importance occurred. If my love's mind was, as Ceneri predicted, to be gradually restored, the process was a tedious one. At times I thought her better—at times worse. The fact is there was little or no change in her condition. Hour after hour she sits in her apathy and listlessness; speaking only when spoken to; but willing to come with me anywhere; do anything I suggest, whenever, alas! I express my wish in words she can comprehend. Poor Pauline!

The greatest doctors in England have seen her. Each says the same thing. She may recover; but each tells me the recovery would be made more possible if the exact circumstances which brought about the calamity were known. These I doubt if we shall ever learn.

For Ceneri has made no sign, nor has Macari sent his promised information. The latter after his last malicious words I dread more than I wish for. Teresa, who might have thrown some light on the subject, has disappeared. I blame myself for not having asked the doctor where she was to be found; but doubtless he would have declined to tell me. So the days go on. All I can do is, with Priscilla's assistance, to ensure that my poor girl is made as happy as can be, and hope that time and care may at length restore her.

We are still at Walpole Street. My intention had been to buy a house and furnish it. But why? Pauline could not look after it—would not be interested in it—it would not be home. So we stay on at my old lodgings and I live almost the life of a hermit.

I care to see no friends. I am, indeed, blamed for forsaking all my old acquaintances. Some who have seen Pauline attribute my lack of hospitality to jealousy; some to other causes; but, as yet, I believe no one knows the truth.

There are times when I feel I cannot bear my grief—times when I wish that Kenyon had never led me inside that church at Turin: but there are other times when I feel that, in spite of all, my love for my wife, hopeless as it is, has made me a better and even a happier man. I can sit for hours looking at her lovely face, even as I could looking at a picture or a statue. I try to imagine that face lit up with bright intelligence, as once it must have been. I long to know what can have drawn that dark curtain over her mind, and I pray that one day it may fall aside and I may see her eyes responsive to my own. If I felt sure this would ever be I would wait without a murmur, if needs be, till our hair has grown grey.

I have this poor consolation—whatever the effect of our marriage may have been upon my life, it has, at least, not made my wife's lot a sadder one. Her days I am sure must be brighter than those when she was under the supervision of that terrible old Italian woman. Priscilla loves her and pets her like a child, whilst I—well, I do everything I can which I fancy may give her such pleasure as she is capable of feeling. Sometimes, not always, she seems to appreciate my efforts, and once or twice she has taken my hand and raised it to her lips as if in gratitude. She is beginning to love me as a child may love its father, as some weak helpless creature may love its protector. This is a poor recompense, but I am thankful even for this.

So, in our quiet household, the days pass by and the months glide away until the winter is over and the laburnums and lilacs in the little plots in front of houses in the suburbs are in bud.

It is fortunate that I am fond of books. Without that taste life would indeed be colourless. I have not the heart to leave Pauline alone and seek society on my own account. I spend my hours every day reading and studying, whilst my wife sits in the same room, silent, unless I address a remark to her.

It is a matter of great grief to me that I am almost entirely debarred from hearing the sound of music. I soon discovered that its effect upon Pauline was prejudicial. The notes which soothed me, in some way seemed to irritate her and make her uneasy. So, unless she is out somewhere with old Priscilla and I am left alone, the piano is unopened; the music books lie unused. Only those who love music as I love it can understand how great a deprivation this is to me.

One morning as I sat alone I was told that a gentleman wished to see me. He gave the servant no name, but instructed her to say that he was from Geneva. I knew it must be Macari. My first impulse was to send back word that I would not see him. Again and again, since our last meeting, his words had come back to me—those words which hinted at something in Pauline's past which her uncle had an object in concealing. But each time I thought of them I discovered they were only the malicious insinuation of a disappointed man, who having failed to win the woman he loved, wished to make his favoured rival suspicious and unhappy. I feared nothing he could say against my wife, but disliking the man, I hesitated before giving instructions for his admittance.

Yet Macari was the only link between Pauline and her past; Ceneri I felt sure I should never see again; this man was the only one remaining from whom it was possible to learn anything respecting my wife. The one person whose appearance could, by any chance, stimulate that torpid memory, and, perhaps, influence the state of her mind by suggesting, no matter how dimly, scenes and events in which he must have played a part. So thinking, I decided that the man should be admitted, and, moreover that he should be brought face to face with Pauline. If he wished to do so he might speak to her of old days, even old passion—anything that might aid her to pick up and retrace those dropped threads of memory.

He entered my room and greeted me with what I knew to be assumed cordiality. I felt, in spite of the hearty grasp he gave my hand, that he meant his visit to bode no good to me. What did I care why he came? I wanted him for a purpose. With the end in view, what mattered the tool, if I could keep it from turning in my hand and wounding me?—and this was to be seen.

I met him with a greeting almost as cordial as his own; I begged him to be seated, then rang for wine and cigars.

'You see I have kept my promise, Mr Vaughan,' he said, with a smile.

'Yes. I trusted you would do so. Have you been long in England?'

'Only a couple of days.'

'How long do you stay?'

'Until I am called abroad again. Things have gone wrong with us there. I must wait until the atmosphere has quietened down.'

I looked at him inquiringly.

'I fancied you knew my trade,' he said. 'I supposed you are a conspirator—I don't use the word offensively; it is the only one I can think of.'

'Yes. Conspirator—regenerator—apostle of freedom, whatever you like.'

'But your country has been free for some years.'

'Other countries are not free. I work for them. Our poor friend Ceneri did the same, but his last day's work is done.'

'Is he dead?' I asked, startled

'Dead to all of us. I cannot give you particulars; but a few weeks after you left Geneva he was arrested in St Petersburg.

He lay in prison for months awaiting his trial. It has come off, I hear.'

'Well, what has happened to him?'

'What always happens—our poor friend is at this moment on his way to Siberia, condemned to twenty years' hard labour in the mines.'

Although I bore no particular love toward Ceneri, I shuddered as I heard his fate.

'And you escaped?' I said.

'Naturally, or I should not be here smoking your very good cigars and sipping your capital claret.'

I was disgusted at the indifference with which he spoke of his friend's misfortune. If it seemed horrible to me to think of the man working in the Siberian mines, what should it have seemed to his fellow conspirator?

'Now, Mr Vaughan,' said the latter, 'with your permission I will enter on business matters with you. I am afraid I shall surprise you.'

'Let me hear what you have to say.'

'First of all I must ask you what Ceneri told you about myself?'

'He told me your name.'

'Nothing of my family? He did not tell you my true name any more than he told you his own? He did not tell you it was March, and that Pauline and I are brother and sister?'

I was astonished at this announcement. In the face of the doctor's assertions that this man had been in love with Pauline, I did not for a moment believe it: but thinking it better to hear his tale out, I simply replied, 'He did not.'

'Very well—then I will tell you my history as briefly as I can. I am known by many names abroad, but my right name is Anthony March. My father and Pauline's married Dr Ceneri's sister. He died young and left the whole of his large property to his wife absolutely. She died some time afterwards, and in turn left everything in my uncle's hands as sole trustee for my sister and myself. You know what became of the money, Mr Vaughan?'

'Dr Ceneri told me,' I said, impressed in spite of myself by the correct way in which he marshalled his facts.

'Yes, it was spent for Italy. It paid for the keep of many a red-shirt, armed many a true Italian. All our fortune was spent by the trustee. I have never blamed him. When I knew where it had gone I freely forgave him.'

'Let us say no more about it, then.'

'I don't quite look upon it in that light. Victor Emmanuel's government is now firmly established. Italy is free and will grow richer every year. Now, Mr Vaughan, my idea is this: I believe, if the facts of the case were laid before the king, something might be done. I believe, if I, and you on behalf of your wife, were to make it known that Ceneri's appropriation of our fortunes for patriotic purposes had left us penniless, a large portion of the money, if not all, would be freely returned to us. You must have friends in England who would assist you in gaining the ear of King Victor. I have friends in Italy. Garibaldi, for instance, would vouch for the amount paid into his hands by Dr Ceneri.'

His tale was plausible, and, after all, his scheme was not altogether visionary.

I was beginning to think he might really be my wife's brother, and that Ceneri had, for some purpose of his own, concealed the relationship.

'But I have plenty of money,' I said.

'But I have not,' he replied with a frank laugh. 'I think you ought for the sake of your wife to join me in the matter.'

'I must take time to consider it.'

'Certainly—I am in no hurry. I will in the meantime get my papers and petition in order. And now may I see my sister?'

'She will be in very shortly if you will wait.'

'Is she better, Mr Vaughan?'

I shook my head sadly.

'Poor girl! then I fear she will not recognize me. We have spent very few days together since we were children. I am, of course, much her senior; and from the age of eighteen have been plotting and fighting. Domestic ties are forgotten under such circumstances.'

I was still far from putting any faith in the man; besides, there were his words on a former occasion to be accounted for.

'Mr Macari,' I said.

'Excuse me—March is my name.'

'Then, Mr March, I must ask you now to tell me the particulars of the shock which deprived my wife of her full reason.'

His face grew grave. 'I cannot now. Some day I will do so.'

'You will then, at least, explain your words when we parted at Geneva?'

'I will ask pardon for them and apologize, as I know I spoke hastily and thoughtlessly—but having forgotten, I am, of course, unable to explain them.'

I said nothing, feeling uncertain whether he was playing a deep game with me or not.

'I know,' he continued, 'that I was furious at hearing of Pauline's marriage. In her state of health Ceneri should never have allowed it—and then, Mr Vaughan, I had set my heart upon her marrying an Italian. Had she recovered, my dream was that her beauty would win her a husband of the highest rank.'

Any reply I should have made was prevented by the entrance of Pauline. I was intensely anxious to see what effect the appearance of her so-called brother would have upon her.

Macari rose and stepped toward her. 'Pauline,' he said, 'do you remember me?'

She looked at him with eyes full of curious wonder, but shook her head as one in doubt. He took her hand. I noticed that she seemed to shrink from him instinctively.

'Poor girl, poor girl!' he said. 'This is worse than I expected, Mr Vaughan. Pauline, it is long since we have met, but you cannot have forgotten me!'

Her large troubled eyes were riveted on his face; but she made no sign of recognition.

'Try and think who it is, Pauline,' I said.

She passed her hand across her forehead, then once more shook her head. '*Non me ricordo,*' she murmured; then, as if the mental effort had exhausted her, sank, with a weary sigh, upon a chair.

I was delighted to hear her speak in Italian. It was a tongue she seldom used unless compelled to do so. That she employed it now showed me she must, in some dim way, connect the visitor with Italy. It was to me a new gleam of hope.

There was another thing I noticed. I have said how seldom it was that Pauline raised her eyes to anyone's face; but today, during the whole time Macari was in the room, she never looked away from him. He sat near her, and after a few more words to her, he addressed his remarks exclusively to me. All the while I could see my wife watching him with an eager, troubled look; several times, indeed, I almost persuaded myself that there was an expression of fear in her eyes. Let them express fear, hate, trouble, even love, so long as I could see the dawn of returning reason in them! I began to think that if Pauline was to be restored, it would be through my visitor.

So when he took his leave I pressed him, with no assumed manner, to call again very soon—tomorrow, if possible. He readily promised to do so, and we parted for the day.

I can only hope he was as satisfied with the result of our interview as I was.

After his departure Pauline fell into a restless state. Several times I saw her pressing her hand to her forehead. She seemed unable to sit still. Now and again she went to the window and looked up and down the street. I paid no attention to her actions, although once or twice I saw her turn her eyes toward me with a piteous, imploring glance. I believed that something—some old memory in connection with Macari—was striving to force itself to her clouded brain, and I looked forward with impatience to tomorrow, when he would pay us another visit. The man had something to get out of me, so I felt certain I should see him again.

He came the next day, and the next, and many other days. It was clear he was determined to ingratiate me, if possible. He did all he could to make himself agreeable, and I must say he was, under the present circumstances, very good company. He knew, or professed to know, all the ins and outs of every plot or political event of the last ten years, and was full of original anecdotes and stirring experiences. He had fought under Garibaldi through the whole of the Italian campaign. He had known the interior of prisons, and some of his escapes from death had been marvellous. I had no reason to doubt the truth of his tales, although I mistrusted the man himself. Let his smile be as pleasant as he could make it—let his laugh ring out naturally—I could not forget the expression I had seen on that face, or his manner and words on former occasions.

I took care that Pauline should always be with us It was the only wish of mine the poor child had ever shown even a mute disinclination to comply with. She never spoke in Macari's presence, but her eyes were scarcely ever turned from him. He seemed to have a kind of fascination for her. When he entered the room I could hear her sigh, and when he left it she breathed a breath of relief; and every day she grew more restless, uneasy, and, I knew, unhappy. My heart smote me as I guessed I was causing her pain; but, at all cost, I determined to persevere. I felt that the crisis of her life was fast drawing near.

One evening, after dinner, as Macari and I sat over our claret, and Pauline, with her troubled eyes fixed as usual on my guest, was reclining on the sofa a little way off, he began to relate some of his military adventures. How once, when in imminent peril—his right arm broken and useless at his side, his left arm not strong enough to wield the rifle with the bayonet fixed—he had taken the bayonet off, and holding it in his left hand, had driven it through the heart of an antagonist. As he described the deed, he suited the gesture to the word, and seizing a knife which lay on the table, dealt a downward blow through the air at an imaginary white-coated Austrian.

I heard a deep sigh behind me, and, turning, I saw Pauline lying with her eyes closed, and apparently in a dead faint. I ran to her, raised her up, and carrying her to her room, laid her on her bed. It was now about nine o'clock. Priscilla happened to be out, so I ran back to the dining-room and bade Macari a hasty good night.

'I hope there is not much the matter,' he said.

'No; only a fainting fit. Your fierce gesture must have frightened her.'

Then I returned to my wife's bedside, and began the usual course of restoratives. Yet without success. White as a statue she lay there, her soft breathing and the faint throb of her pulse only telling that she was alive. She lay there without sense or motion, while I chafed her hands, bathed her brow, and endeavoured to recall her to life. Even whilst doing so my heart was beating wildly. I felt that the moment had come; that something had brought back the past to her, and that the fierce rush with which it came had overpowered her. I could scarcely dare to put my wild belief into words, but it was that when Pauline again opened her eyes they would shine with light which I had never known in them—the light of perfectly restored intelligence. A wild, mad idea, but one I had the fullest faith in.

So it was that I did not send for a doctor; that after a while I gave up my own attempts to awaken consciousness; that I resolved to let her lie in that calm, senseless state until she awoke of her own accord. I took her wrist between my fingers, that I might feel every beat of her pulse. I laid my cheek against hers, that I might catch the sound of every breath—and thus I waited until Pauline should awake, and, as I fondly believed, awake in her right mind.

She remained in this state for at least an hour. So long that at last I began to get frightened, and think I must, after all, send for medical aid. Just as I was forming the resolution to do so, I noticed the beats of her pulse grow stronger and more rapid; I felt her breath drawn deeper; I saw a look of returning life steal over her face; and, in breathless impatience, I waited.

And then Pauline—my wife—came back to life. She rose in the bed and turned her face to mine; and in her eves I saw what, by the mercy of God, I shall never again see there!

CHAPTER VIII

CALLED BACK

I WRITE this chapter with great reluctance. If I could make my tale connected and complete without it, I should prefer to say nothing about the events it records. If some of my experiences have been strange ones, all save these can be explained; but these never will, never can be explained to my satisfaction.

Pauline awoke, and, as I saw her eyes, I shuddered as if a freezing wind had passed over me. It was not madness I saw in them, neither was it sense. They were dilated to the utmost extent; they were fixed and immovable, yet I knew they saw absolutely nothing; that their nerves conveyed no impression to the brain. All my wild hopes that reason would return at the expiration of her fainting fit, were at an end. It was clear that she had passed into a state far more pitiable than her former one.

I spoke to her; called her by name; but she took no notice of my words. She seemed to be unaware of my presence. She looked ever, with strange fixed eyes, in one direction.

Suddenly she rose, and, before I could interpose to prevent her, passed out of the room. I followed her. She went swiftly down the stairs, and I saw she was making for the front door. Her hand was on the latch when I came up to her and again called her by name; entreating, even commanding her to return. No sound of my voice seemed to reach her ears. In her critical state, for so I felt it to be, I shrank from restraining her by force, thinking it would be better to leave her free to go as she listed; of course accompanying her to guard her against evil.

I caught up my hat and a large cloak, both of which were hanging in the hall; the latter I wrapped around her as she walked, and managed to draw the hood over her head. She made no resistance to this, but she let me do it without a word to show that she noticed the action. Then, with me at her side, she walked straight on.

She went at a swift but uniform pace, as one who had a certain destination in view. She turned her eyes neither to the left nor right—neither up nor down. Not once during that walk did I see them move, not once did I see an eyelid quiver. Although my sleeve was touching hers, I am certain she had no thought or knowledge of my presence.

I made no further attempt to check her progress. She was not wandering about in an aimless manner. Something, I knew not what, was guiding or impelling her steps to some set purpose. Something in her disordered brain was urging her to reach some spot as quickly as possible. I dreaded the consequences of restraining her from so doing. Even if it was but an exaggerated case of sleep-walking it would be unwise to wake her. Far better to follow her until the fit ended.

She passed out of Walpole Street, and, without a moment's hesitation, turned at right angles and went along the straight broad road. Along this road for more than half a mile she led me, then, turning sharply round, walked half-way through another street, then she stopped before a house.

An ordinary three-storey house of the usual London type. A house differing very little from my own and thousands of others, except that, by the light of the street lamp, I could see it looked ill-cared for and neglected. The window panes were dusty, and in one of them was a bill stating that this desirable residence was to let, furnished.

I marvelled as to what strange freak of mind could have led Pauline to this untenanted house. Had anyone she had known in former days lived here? If so, it was, perhaps, a hopeful sign that some awakened memory had induced her to direct her unwitting steps to a place associated with her earlier days. Very anxious, and even much excited, I waited to see what course she would now take.

She went straight up to the door and laid her hand upon it, as though she expected it would yield to her touch. Then, for the first time, she seemed to hesitate and grow troubled.

'Pauline, dearest,' I said, 'let us go back now. It is dark, and too late to go in there tonight. Tomorrow, if you like, we will come again.'

She answered not. She stood before that door with her hand pressing against it. I took her arm, and tried gently to lead her away. She resisted with a passive strength I should not have believed she possessed. Whatever was the dimly conceived object in my poor wife's brain, it was plain to me it could only be attained by passing through that door.

I was quite willing to humour her. Having come so far, I feared to retreat. To cross her wishes in the present state of things I felt might be fatal. But how could we gain entrance?

There was no gleam of light upstairs or downstairs. As you looked at the house you knew intuitively it was uninhabited. The agent whose name appeared on the bill carried on business a mile away, and, even if I had ventured to leave Pauline and go in search of him, at this time of night my expedition would be fruitless.

As I cast around, wondering what was the best thing to do—whether to fetch a cab and carry my poor girl into it, or whether to let her wait here until she recognized the impossibility of entering the house and, at last growing weary, choose to return home of her own accord—as I debated these alternatives a sudden thought struck me. Once before my latchkey had opened a strange door, it was within the bounds of possibility it might do so again. I knew that uninhabited houses are often, from carelessness or convenience, left with doors only latched. It was an absurd idea, but, after all, there was no harm in trying. I drew out my key, a duplicate of that used on another occasion.

I placed it in the keyhole without a hope of success, and, as I felt the lock turn and saw the door yield, a thrill of something like horror ran through me, for now that it had come to pass I knew this thing could be no mere coincidence.

As the door opened, Pauline, without a word, without a gesture of surprise, without anything that showed she was more aware of my presence than before, passed me and entered first. I followed her, and, closing the door behind me, found myself in perfect darkness. I heard her light quick step in front of me; I heard her ascending the stairs; I heard a door open, and then, and only then, I summoned up presence of mind enough to force my limbs to bear me in pursuit—and my blood seemed to be iced water, my flesh was creeping, my hair was bristling up, as, still in darkness, I crossed the hall and found the staircase without difficulty.

Why should I not find it, dark, pitch dark as it was? I knew the road to it well! Once before I had reached it in darkness, and many times besides, in dreams, had I crossed that space! Like a sudden revelation the truth came to me. It came to me as the key turned in the lock. I was in that very house into which I had strayed three years ago. I was crossing the very hall, ascending the same stairs, and should stand in the identical room which had been the scene of that terrible unexpiated crime. I should see with restored sight the spot where, blind and helpless, I had nearly fallen a victim to my rashness. But Pauline, what brought her here?

Yes, as I expected! As, in fact, I felt certain! The stairs the same and the lintel of the door in the exact place it should be. I might be reacting the events of that fearful night, complete even to the darkness. For a moment I wondered whether the last three years were not the dream; whether I was not blind now; whether there was such a being as my wife? But I threw the fancy aside.

Where was Pauline? Recalled to myself, I realized the necessity of light. Drawing my match-box from my pocket

I struck a Vesta, and by its light I entered the room which once before I had entered with little hope of ever leaving.

My first thought, my first glance, was for Pauline. She was there, standing erect in the apartment, with both hands pressed to her brow. The expression of her face and eyes was little changed; it was easy to see she comprehended nothing as yet. But I felt that something was struggling within her, and I dreaded the moment when it should take coherence and form. I dreaded it for her and I dreaded it for myself. What awful passages would it reveal to me?

The wax light burnt down to my fingers, and I was compelled to drop it. I struck another, then looked about for some means of making the illumination sustained. To my great joy I found a half-burnt candle in a candlestick on the mantelpiece. I blew the thick dust out of the cup formed by the melted wax at the bottom of the wick, and after a little spluttering and resistance, managed to induce it to remain lighted.

Pauline stood always in the same attitude, but I fancied her breath was quickening. Her fingers were playing convulsively round her temples, fidgeting and pushing her thick hair back, striving, it seemed to me, to conjure thought to return to that empty shrine. I could do nothing but wait; and while I waited I glanced around me.

We were in a good-sized room, substantially but not fashionably furnished; the style altogether was that of an ordinary lodging house. It was clear it had not been occupied for some time, as dust lay thick on every article. I could throw my mind back and recall the very corner of the room in which I was stationed while the assassins were so busily engaged. I could mark the spot where I fell upon the yet quivering body, and I shuddered as I could not resist peering on the floor for traces of the crime. But if the carpet was the same one, it was of a dark red hue and kept its secret well. At one end of the room were folding doors—it must have been from behind these I heard those haunting sounds of distress. I threw them open, and, holding my candle on high, looked in. The room was of much the same kind as the other one, but, as I fully expected, it contained a piano—the very piano, perhaps, whose notes had merged into that cry of horror.

What possessed me! What impulse urged me! I shall never know. I laid down the candle; I entered the back room; I lifted the dust-covered lid of the piano and I struck a few notes. Doubtless it was the tragical associations of the scene which made me, without thinking why or wherefore, blend together the notes which commenced that great song which I had heard as I lingered outside the door, listening to the sweet voice singing, and wondering whose voice it was. As I struck those notes I looked through the folding door at the motionless, statue-like figure of Pauline.

A nervous trembling seemed to pass over her frame. She turned and came toward me, and there was a look in her face which made me move aside from the piano, and wonder and fear what was to take place.

The cloak I had thrown around her had fallen from her shoulders. She seated herself on the music bench, and striking the keys with a master hand, played brilliantly and faultlessly the prelude to the song of which I had struck a few vagrant notes.

I was thunderstruck. Never till now had she shown the slightest taste for music—as I have said, it appeared rather to annoy and irritate her. Now she was bringing out sounds which it seemed absurd to expect from that neglected and untuned piano.

But after the first few bars my astonishment ceased. As well as if I had been told, I knew what would happen—or part of it. I was even prepared, when the moment came for the voice to join the music, to hear Pauline sing as faultlessly as she was playing, yet to sing in the same subdued manner as on that fatal night. So fully prepared I was, that with breathless emotion I waited until the song came to the very note at which it finished when once before I listened to it. So fully prepared, that when she started wildly to her feet and uttered once more that cry of horror, my arms were round her in a moment, and I bore her to a sofa close by.

To her, as well as to me, all the occurrences of that dreadful night were being reproduced. The past had come back to Pauline—come back at the moment it left her.

What the reflux might do eventually—whether it would be a blessing or a curse—I had no time to consider. All my cares were needed by Pauline. My task was terrible! I had to hold her down by main force, to endeavour in every possible way to soothe her and prevent her cries, which rang so loudly that I feared the neighbours would be alarmed. And all the while she struggled with me, strove to repulse me and regain her feet; as certainly as if I could read her thoughts, I knew that whatever had happened formerly was once more before her eyes. Once more she was being held down by a strong hand, most likely on the same couch, and once more her struggles were gradually becoming feebler and her cries growing fainter. It needed only for the latter to sink at last into a repetition of that dismal moan to make the picture, so far as she was concerned, complete. The only difference was that the hands now laid upon her were loving ones.

All things up to the present situation, and all that I narrate after the termination of this chapter, I expect to be believed. I do not say that such events and coincidences are of everyday occurrence. Had they been so, I should have no object in writing this tale. But I do say this, all else save this one thing I could prove to be true, if not by direct by circumstantial evidence; all else can be explained either simply or scientifically; but what follows I can only give my own word for. Call it what you like, dream, hallucination, overheated imagination—call it anything save invention—I shall not be annoyed. This is what happened.

Pauline at last lay still. Her moan had sunk into silence. She seemed once more to have lost all consciousness. My one idea now was to remove her as speedily as possible from this fatal place. All sorts of strange thoughts and speculations were thronging my brain. All sorts of hopes and fears were shaking me. What would the explanation be, if ever I could get it?

My poor darling lay still and peaceful. I thought I would let her rest so for a few moments before I carried her out. I dreaded what waking her might mean. So I took her hand and held it close in mine.

The candle was on the mantelpiece behind me. It threw little or no light into the front room, the folding doors of which were only partially open—the half behind the couch on which Pauline lay being closed. It was, therefore, impossible for me from my seat beside her to look into the front room. Indeed, as I sat there my face was turned from it.

I held my wife's hand for a few seconds, and then a strange undefinable feeling crept over me—the kind of feeling some-times experienced in a dream in which two persons appear, and the dreamer cannot be certain with which one's thoughts and acts he identifies himself. For a while I seemed to have a dual existence. Although perfectly aware that I still occu-pied the same seat, still held Pauline's hand in mine, I was also seated at the piano, and in some way gazed through the half-opened doors into the other room, and that room was full of light!

Light so brilliant that in a glance I could see everything the apartment contained. Each article of furniture, the pictures on the walls, the dark curtains drawn over the window at the end, the mirror over the fireplace, the table in the centre, on which a large lamp was burning. I could see all this, and more! For round the table were grouped four men, and the faces of two of the party were well known to me!

That man who was facing me—leaning across the table on which his hands rested, whose features seemed full of alarmed surprise, whose eyes were fixed on one object a few feet away from him—that man was Ceneri, the Italian doctor, Pauline's uncle and guardian.

That man who was near the table on Ceneri's right hand—who stood in the attitude of one ready to repel a possible attack, whose face was fierce and full of passion, whose dark eyes were blazing—that man was the English-speaking Italian, Macari, or, as he now styled himself, Anthony March, Pauline's brother. He also was looking at the same object as Ceneri.

The man in the background—a short, thick-set man with a scar on his cheek—was a stranger to me. He was looking over Ceneri's shoulder in the same direction.

And the object they all looked at was a young man, who appeared to be falling out of his chair, and whose hand grasped convulsively the hilt of a dagger, the blade of which was buried in his heart, buried I knew by a blow which had been struck downward by one standing over him.

All this I saw and realized in a second. The attitude of each actor, the whole scene surrounding was taken in by me as one takes in with a single glance the purpose and meaning of a picture. Then I dropped Pauline's hand and sprang to my feet.

Where was the lighted room? Where were the figures I had seen? Where was that tragic scene which was taking place before my eyes? Vanished into thin air! The candle was burning dimly behind me, the front room was in dusk. Pauline and I were the only living creatures in the place!

It was a dream, of course. Perhaps, under the circumstances, not an unnatural one. Knowing what I knew already of the crime which had taken place here; feeling sure that in some way Pauline had been present when it was committed; excited by what had occurred tonight—Pauline's strange walk, her sudden bursting into song, the very song I had before heard, that song with the dreadful ending—it is no wonder that I imagined a scene like this, and taking the only persons I knew who were in any way connected with my poor wife, brought them into the life-like vision.

But given that a man may dream the same dream twice, perhaps three times, there is no record of his dreaming it as often as he willed. Yet this was my case. Again I took Pauline's hand, and again, after a few moments' waiting, I felt the same strange sensation and saw the same awful sight. Not once, not twice, but many times did this occur, until, sceptical as I was, as even I am now in such matters, I could only believe that in some mysterious way I was actually gazing on the very sight which had met the girl's eyes when memory, perhaps mercifully, fled from her, and reason was left impaired.

It was only when our hands were in contact that the scene came before me. This fact strengthened my theory. I felt then—I feel now, it is the true one. What peculiar mental or physical organization can have brought about such an effect I am unable to say. Call it cataleptic, clairvoyant, anything you will, but it was as I relate.

Again and again I took Pauline's hand, and as I held it looked into that brilliantly lighted room.

Like the motionless figures in a *tableau vivant*, again and again, without a change of attitude or expression, I saw Ceneri, Macari, and the man in the background looking at their victim. The appearance of the last-named I studied very closely. Even with the agony of death on his face I could see he was supremely handsome. His must have been a face that women love to look upon, and even through the horror of the vision, a painful thought came to me as I wondered what might have been his relations with the girl who saw him suddenly struck down.

Who had struck him? Without a doubt Macari, who, as I said, was standing nearest to him, in the attitude of one expecting an attack. His hand might just have quitted the dagger hilt. His downward stroke had driven the blade so deeply into the heart that death and the blow were all but simultaneous. This was what Pauline saw, what perhaps she was seeing now, and what, by some strange power, she was able to show me as one shows another a picture!

Ever since that night I have wondered how I found the presence of mind to sit there and repeatedly call up, by the aid of that senseless girl by my side, that phantasmagoria It must have been the burning desire to fathom the mysteries of that long past night, the wish to learn exactly what shock had disarranged my wife's intellect, the indignation I felt at the cowardly murder, and the hope of bringing the criminals to justice, which gave me strength to produce and reproduce that scene until I was satisfied that I knew all that dumb show could tell me, until my heart smote me for letting Pauline lie so long in her present state.

Then I wrapped her cloak around her, raised her in my arms and bore her from the room, down the stairs to the door. The hour was not late; I soon, by the aid of a passer-by, summoned a cab, and in a very short time reached home, and laid her, still insensible, upon her bed.

Whatever strange power she had possessed of communicating her thoughts to me, it ceased as soon as we were outside that fatal house. Now and hereafter I could hold her hand, but no dream, vision, or hallucination followed the act.

This is the one thing I cannot explain—the mystery at which I hinted when I commenced my tale. I have related what happened; if my bare word is insufficient to win credence, I must be content on this one point to be disbelieved.

CHAPTER IX

A BLACK LIE

HAVING placed the poor girl in Priscilla's motherly hands, I fetched the best doctor I could think of, and efforts were at once made to restore consciousness. It was long before any sign of returning animation showed itself, but, at last, she awoke. Need I say what a supreme moment that was to me?

I need not give details of that return to life. After all, it was but a half return, and brought fresh terrors in its train. When morning dawned it found Pauline raving with what I prayed was but the delirium of fever.

The doctor told me her state was a most critical one. There was hope for her life, but no certainty of saving it. It was during those days of anxiety that I learned how much I loved my unhappy girl. How grateful I should be if she were given back to me, even as I had always known her.

Her wild fevered words cut me to the heart. Sometimes in English, sometimes in soft Italian, she called on someone; spoke words of deep love and sorrow; gave vent to expressions of fond endearment. These were succeeded by cries of grief, and it seemed as if shudders of fear passed over her.

For me there was no word; no look of recognition. I, who would have given worlds to hear my name spoken once, during her delirium, with an expression of love, was but a stranger at her bedside.

Whom was it she called for and lamented? Who was the man that she and I had seen slain? I soon learned—and if my informant spoke the truth, he had, in so doing, dealt me a blow from which I should never rally.

It was Macari who struck it. He called on me the day after Pauline and I had visited that house. I would not see him then. My plans were not formed. For the time I could think of nothing save my wife's danger. But two days afterward, when he again called, I gave orders for him to be admitted.

I shuddered as I took the hand I dared not yet refuse him, although in my own mind I was certain that a murderer's fingers were clasped round my own. Perhaps the very fingers which had once closed on my throat. Yet, with all I knew, I doubted whether I could bring him to justice.

Unless Pauline recovered, the evidence I could bring would be of no weight. Even the victim's name was unknown to me. Before the accusation would lie his remains must be found and identified. It was hopeless to think of punishing the murderer, now that more than three years had elapsed since the crime.

Besides—was he Pauline's brother?

Brother or not, I would unmask him. I would show him that the crime was no longer a secret; that an outsider knew every detail. I would tell him this in the hope that his future would be haunted with the dread of a just vengeance overtaking him.

I knew the name of the street to which Pauline had led me. I had noticed it as we drove from it a few nights ago, and the reason of my drunken guide's mistake was apparent. It was Horace Street. My conductor had jumbled up Walpole and Horace in his drink-muddled brain.

On what a slight thread the whole course of a life hangs!

Macari had heard of Pauline's illness and delirium. He was as tenderly solicitous in his inquiries as a brother should be. My replies were cold and brief. Brother or not, he was answerable for everything.

Presently he changed the subject. 'I scarcely like to trouble you at such a time, but I should be glad to know if you are willing to join me, as I suggested, in a memorial to Victor Emmanuel?'

'I am not. There are several things I must have explained first.'

He bowed politely; but I saw his lips close tightly for a moment.

'I am quite at your service,' he said.

'Very well. Before all I must be satisfied that you are my wife's brother.'

He raised his thick, dark eyebrows and tried to smile.

'That is easily done. Had poor Ceneri been with us, he would have vouched for it.'

'But he told me very differently.'

'Ah, he had his reasons. No matter, I can bring plenty of other persons.'

'Then, again,' I said, looking him full in the face and speaking very slowly, 'I must know why you murdered a man three years ago in a house in Horace Street.'

Whichever the fellow felt—fear or rage—the expression of his face was that of blank astonishment. Not, I knew, the surprise of innocence, but of wonder that the crime should be known. For a moment his jaw dropped and he gaped at me in silence.

Then he recovered. 'Are you mad, Mr Vaughan?' he cried.

'On the 20th of August, 186—, at No. — Horace Street, you stabbed to the heart a young man who was sitting at the table. Dr Ceneri was in the room at the time, also another man with a scar on his face.'

He attempted no evasion. He sprang to his feet with features convulsed with rage. He seized my arm. For a moment I thought he meant to attack me, but found he only wanted to scan my face attentively. I did not shrink from his inspection. I hardly thought he would recognize me, so great a change does blindness make in a face.

But he knew me. He dropped my arm and stamped his foot in fury.

'Fools! Idiots!' he hissed. 'Why did they not let me do the work thoroughly?'

He walked once or twice up and down the room, and then with regained composure stood in front of me.

'You are a great actor, Mr Vaughan,' he said, with a coolness and cynicism which appalled me. 'You deceived even me, and I am very suspicious.'

'You do not even deny the crime, you villain?'

He shrugged his shoulders. 'Why should I, to an eye-witness? To others I will deny it fast enough. Besides, as you are interested in the matter, there is no occasion to do so.'

'I am interested!'

'Certainly; as you married my sister. Now, my fine fellow! my gay bridegroom! my dear brother-in-law! I will tell you why I killed that man and what I meant by my words to you at Geneva.'

His air of bitter, callous mockery, as he spoke these words, made me dread what was to come. My hands were tingling to throw him from the room.

'That man—I shall not for obvious reasons tell you his name—was Pauline's lover. Translate "lover" into Italian—into what the word *drudo* signifies in that language—then you will understand my meaning. We, on our mother's side have noble blood in our veins—blood which brooks no insult. He was Pauline's, your wife's, lover, I say again. He had no wish to marry her, and so Ceneri and I killed him—killed him in London—even in her presence. As I told you once before, Mr Vaughan, it is well to marry a woman who cannot recall the past.'

I made no reply. So hideous a statement called for no comment. I simply rose and walked toward him

He saw my purpose written in my face. 'Not here,' he said hastily, and moving away from me: 'what good can it do here—a vulgar scuffle between two gentlemen? No; on the Continent—anywhere, meet me, and I will show you how I hate you.'

He spoke well, the self-possessed villain! What good could it do? An unseemly struggle, in which I could scarcely hope to kill him; and Pauline the while perhaps upon the point of death!

'Go,' I cried, 'murderer and coward! Every word you have ever spoken to me has been a lie, and because you hate me, you have today told me the greatest lie of all. Go; save yourself from the gallows by flight.'

He gave me a look of malicious triumph and left me. The air in the room seemed purer now that he no longer breathed it.

Then I went to Pauline's room, and sitting by her bed heard her parched lips ever and ever calling in English or Italian on someone she loved. Heard them beseeching and warning, and knew that her wild words were addressed to the man whom Macari averred he had slain because he was the lover of his sister—my wife!

The villain lied! I knew he lied. Over and over again I told myself it was a black, slanderous lie—that Pauline was as pure as an angel. But, as I strove to comfort myself with these assertions, I knew that, lie as it was, until I could prove it such, it would rankle in my heart; would be ever with me; would grow until I mistook it for truth; would give me not a moment's rest or peace, until it made me curse the day when Kenyon led me inside that old church to see 'the fairest sight of all'.

How could I prove the untruth? There were but two other persons in the world who knew Pauline's history—Ceneri and old Teresa. Teresa had disappeared and Ceneri was in the Siberian mines or some other living grave. Even as I thought of the old Italian woman, Macari's slander began to throw forth its first poisonous shoots. Her mysterious words, 'not for love or marriage', might bear another meaning, a dishonourable meaning. And other circumstances would come to me: Ceneri's haste to get his niece married—his wish to get rid of her. Thoughts of this sort would steal into my mind until they half-maddened me.

I could bear to sit with Pauline no longer. I went out into the open air and wandered about aimlessly, until two ideas occurred to me. One was that I would go to the greatest authority on brain diseases, and consult him as to Pauline's hope of recovery—the other that I would go to Horace Street and examine, by daylight, the house from top to bottom. I went first to the doctor's.

To him I told everything, saving, of course, Macari's black lie. I could see no other way to explain the case without confiding fully. I most certainly succeeded in arousing his interest. He had already seen Pauline and knew exactly the state in which she had been. I think he believed, as many others will, all I told him except that one strange occurrence. Even this he did not scoff at, accustomed as he was to wild fancies and freaks of imagination. He attributed it to this cause which was but natural. And now what comfort or hope could he give me?

'As I told you before, Mr Vaughan,' he said, 'such a thing as losing the recollection of the past for a long while and then picking up the end of the thread where it fell is not altogether unprecedented. I will come and see your wife; but as the case now stands it seems to me it is an attack of brain fever, and as yet no specialist is needed. When that fever leaves her I should like to know, that I may see her. It will, I expect, leave her sane, but she will begin life again from the hour that her mind was first unhinged. You, her husband, may even be as a stranger to her. The case, I say again, is not unprecedented, but the circumstances which surround it are.'

I left the doctor and walked to the agents in whose hands the house in Horace Street was placed. I obtained the keys and made some inquiries. I found that at the time of the murder the house had been let furnished for a few weeks to an Italian gentleman whose name was forgotten. He had paid the rent in advance, so no inquiries had been made about him. The house had been vacant for a long time. There was nothing against it except that the owner would only let it at a certain rent, which most people appeared to consider too high.

I gave my name and address and took the keys. I spent the remainder of the afternoon in searching every nook and cranny in the house, but no discovery rewarded my labour. There was, I believed, no place in which the body of a victim could have been hid—there was no garden in which it might have been buried. I took back the keys and said the house did not suit me. Then I returned home and brooded on my grief, whilst Macari's lie ate and ate its way to my heart.

And day by day it went on working and gnawing, corroding and warping, until I was told that the crisis was over; that Pauline was out of danger; that she was herself again.

Which self? The self I had only known, or the self before that fatal night? With a beating heart I drew near to her bedside. Weak, exhausted, without strength to move or speak she opened her eyes and looked at me. It was a look of wonder, of non-recognition, but it was the look of restored reason. She knew me not. It was as the doctor had predicted. I might have been a total stranger to those beautiful eyes as they opened, gazed at me, and then reclosed themselves wearily. I went from the room with tears running down my cheeks, and at my heart a feeling of mingled joy and sorrow, hope and fear, which words will not express.

Then Macari's black lie came out from its lurking place and seized me as it were by the throat—clung to me, wrestled with me—cried, 'I am true! Push me away, I am still true. The lips of a villain spoke to me, but for once he spoke the truth. If not for this, why the crime? Men do not lightly commit murder.' Even then when the moment I had prayed and longed for had come—when sense, full sense, was given back to my poor love—I was invaded, conquered, and crushed to the ground by the foul lie which might be truth.

'We are strangers—she knows me not,' I cried. 'Let me prove that this lie is a lie or let us be strangers for ever!'

How could I prove it? How could I ask Pauline? Or asking her, how could I expect her to answer? Even if she did, would her word satisfy me? Oh that I could see Ceneri! Villain he might be, but I felt he was not such a double-dyed villain as Macari.

Thinking thus, I formed a desperate resolve. Men are urged to do strange and desperate things when life is at stake—with me it was more than life. It was the honour, the happiness— everything of two people.

Yes, I would do it! Mad as the scheme seemed, I would go to Siberia, and if money, perseverance, favour, or craft could bring me face to face with Ceneri, I would wring the truth, the whole truth from his lips!

CHAPTER X

IN SEARCH OF THE TRUTH

ACROSS Europe—half-way across Asia—for the sake of an hour's interview with a Russian political prisoner! It was a wild scheme, but I was determined to carry it out. If my plan was a mad one, I would, at least, ensure a chance of its success by putting all the method I could in my preparations. I would not rush wildly to my journey's end and find it rendered fruitless by the stupidity or suspicion of someone vested with brief authority. No; I must go armed with credentials which no one would dare to dispute. Money, one of the most important of all, I had plenty of, and was ready to use freely; but there were others which were indispensable; my first step would be to obtain these. I could go quietly and systematically to work, for it would be days before I could venture to leave Pauline. Only when all chance of danger was at an end could I begin my journey.

So during those days whilst the poor girl was gradually, but very, very slowly, regaining strength, I looked up what friends I possessed among the great people of the land, until I found one whose position was such that he could ask a favour of a far greater man than himself, and, moreover, expect that it should be granted without delay. He did this for my sake with such efficacy that I received a letter of introduction to the English ambassador at St Petersburg, and also the copy of a letter which had been forwarded him containing instructions on my behalf. Each of the letters bore an autograph which would ensure every assistance being given to me. With these, and the addition of a letter of credit for a large amount on a St Petersburg bank, I was ready to start.

But before I left, Pauline's safety and well-being during these months of absence must be considered. The difficulties this presented almost made me abandon, or, at least, postpone, the execution of my plan. Yet I knew it must be carried out to the very letter, or Macari's lie would ever stand between my wife and myself. Better I should go at once, while we were strangers; better, if Ceneri by word or silence confirmed the shameful tale, that we should never meet again!

Pauline would be left in good hands. Priscilla would do my bidding faithfully and fully. The old woman was by this time quite aware that her charge had awakened to both memory and new forgetfulness. She knew the reason why for days and days I had not even entered the room. She knew that I considered Pauline, in her present state, no more my wife than when I first met her in Turin. She knew that some mystery was attached to our relations with each other, and that I was bound upon a long journey to clear this up. She was content with this knowledge, or sought to obtain no more than I chose to give her.

My instructions were minute. As soon as she was well enough Pauline was to be taken to the seaside. Everything was to be done for her comfort and according to her wishes. If she grew curious she was to be told that some near relation, who was now journeying abroad, had placed her in Priscilla's hands, where she was to stay until his return. But, unless the recollection of the past few months came to her, she was to be told nothing as to her true position as my wife. Indeed, I doubted now if she was legally my wife—whether, if she wished, she might not annul the marriage by stating that at the time it took place she was not in her right mind. When I returned from my expedition—if things were right, as I told myself they must be, all would have to be begun again from the beginning.

I had ascertained that, since the departure of the fever, Pauline had said nothing about the terrible deed she had witnessed three years ago. I feared that when her health was re-established her first wish would be to make some stir in the matter. It was hard to see what she could possibly do. Macari, I learned, had left England the day after I accused him of crime; Ceneri was out of reach. I hoped that Pauline might be induced to remain quiet until my return; and I instructed Priscilla, in the event of her recurring to the subject of a great crime committed by persons she knew, to inform her that all was being done to bring the guilty to their deserts. I trusted she would, with her usual docility, rest contented with this scarcely correct assertion.

Priscilla was to write to me—to St Petersburg, Moscow, and other places I must stop at, going and returning. I left directed envelopes with her, and would send from St Petersburg instructions as to the dates when the various letters should be posted. And then all I could think of was done.

All except one thing. Tomorrow morning I must start. My passport is duly signed; my trunks are packed—everything ready. Once, once for a moment I must see her before I sleep tonight—see her it may be for the last time. She was sleeping soundly—Priscilla told me so. Once more I must look upon that beautiful face that I may carry its exact image with me for thousands of miles!

I crept upstairs and entered her room. I stood by the bedside and gazed with eyes full of tears on my wife—yet not my wife. I felt like a criminal, a desecrator, so little right, I knew, I had to be in that room. Her pale pure face lay on the pillow—the fairest face in all the world to me. Her bosom rose and fell with her soft regular breathing. Fair and white as an angel she looked, and I swore, as I gazed on her, that no word of man should make me doubt her innocence. Yet I would go to Siberia.

I would have given worlds for the right to lay my lips on hers! to have been able to awake her with a kiss, and see those long dark lashes rise, and her eyes beam with love for me. Even as it was I could not refrain from kissing her gently on the temple, just where the soft thick hair began to grow. She stirred in her sleep, her eyelids quivered, and like one detected at the commencement of a crime, I fled.

The next day I was hundreds of miles away, and my mind was in a sterner frame. If when I reached, if ever I did reach, Ceneri, I found that Macari had not lied—found that I had been fooled, made a tool of, I should, at least, have the grim consolation of revenge. I should be able to gloat upon the misery of the man who had deceived me and used me for his own purposes. I should see him dragging out his wretched life in chains and degradation. I should see him a slave, beaten and ill-treated. If this was the only reward I should reap, it would repay me for my long journey. Perhaps, considering all that had passed and my present anxiety and dread, this unchristian state of mind was not unnatural to an ordinary son of Adam.

St Petersburg at last! The letter I bear, and the letter already received on my account, ensure me a gracious reception from her majesty's noble representative in the Russian capital. My request is listened to attentively; not scouted as ridiculous. I am told it is unprecedented, but the words impossible to be granted are not used. There are difficulties, great difficulties, in the way, but, as my business is purely of a domestic nature, with no political tendency, and as the letters bear the magic autograph of a person whom the noble lord is eager to oblige, I am not told that the obstacles are insuperable. I must wait patiently for days, it may be weeks, but I can be sure that everything will be done that can be done. There is, at present, or so the newspapers say, a little friction between the two Governments. Sometimes this is shown by requests more simple than mine being refused. Still, we shall see—

Meanwhile, who is the prisoner, and where is he?

Ah! that I cannot say. I only know him as a doctor named Ceneri—an Italian—an apostle of freedom—patriot—conspirator.

I was not foolish enough to imagine he had been tried and sentenced under the name I knew him by. I supposed this to be a false one.

Lord —— was certain that no one of that name has been sentenced within the last few months. That mattered little. Permission accorded, with the data I had given, the man would at once be identified by the police. Now, good morning—as soon as possible I should hear from the embassy.

'And one word of caution, Mr Vaughan,' said his lordship. 'You are not in England. Remember that a hasty word, even a look; a casual remark to any stranger you sit next at dinner, may utterly defeat your ends. The system of government here is different from ours.'

I thanked him for his advice, although I needed no warning. The truth is that an Englishman in Russia has an even exaggerated dread of spies and the consequences of a loose tongue. More of us are looked upon with suspicion from our taciturnity than from our garrulity. I was not likely to err on the latter point.

I went back to my hotel, and for the next few days whiled away the time as best I could. Not that, under ordinary circumstances, I should have found much difficulty in so doing. St Petersburg was one of the places I had always wished to visit. Its sights were new and strange to me; its customs worth studying; but I took little interest in anything I saw. I was longing to be away in pursuit of Ceneri.

I was not foolish enough to pester the ambassador and make myself a nuisance. Believing he would do all he could, I waited patiently and in silence until I received a letter asking me to call at the embassy. Lord —— received me kindly.

'It is all settled,' he said. 'You will go to Siberia armed with authority which the most ignorant gaoler or soldier will recognize. Of course, I have pledged my honour that in no way will you connive at the convict's escape—that your business is purely private.'

I expressed my thanks, and asked for instructions.

'First of all,' he said, 'my instructions are to take you to the palace. The Czar desires to see the eccentric Englishman who wishes to make such a long journey in order to ask a few questions.'

I would right willingly have declined the honour, but as there was no chance of escaping from it, nerved myself to meet the autocrat as well as I could. The ambassador's carriage was at the door, and in a few minutes we were driven to the Imperial Palace.

I retain a confused recollection of gigantic sentries, glittering officers, grave-looking ushers and other officials; noble staircases and halls; paintings, statues, tapestry and gilding; then, following my conductor, I entered a large apartment, at one end of which stood a tall noble-looking man in military attire; and I realized that I was in the presence of him whose nod could sway millions and millions of his fellow-creatures—the Emperor of all the Russias—the White Czar Alexander II—the sovereign whose rule stretches from the highest civilization of Europe to the lowest barbarism of Asia.

Two years ago when the news of his cruel death reached England, I thought of him as l saw him that day—in the prime of life, tall, commanding and gracious—a man it does one good to look at. Whether—if the whole truth of his great ancestor Catherine the Second's frailties were known—the blood of a peasant or a king ran in his veins, he looked every inch a ruler of men, a splendid despot.

To me he was particularly kind and condescending. His manner set me as much at my ease as it is possible for a man to be in such august company. Lord —— presented me by name, and after a proper reverence I waited the Czar's commands.

He looked at me for a second from his towering height. Then he spoke to me in French, fluently and without much foreign accent:

'I am told you wish to go to Siberia?'

'With your Majesty's gracious permission.'

'To see a political prisoner. Is that so?'

I replied in the affirmative.

'It is a long journey for such a purpose.'

'My business is of the most vital importance, your Majesty.'

'Private importance, I understand from Lord ——.'

He spoke in a quick, stern way which showed that he admitted of no prevarication. I hastened to assure him of the purely private nature of my desired interview with the criminal.

'Is he a dear friend of yours?'

'Rather, an enemy, your Majesty; but my happiness and my wife's happiness are at stake.'

He smiled at my explanation. 'You English are good to your wives. Very well, Mr Vaughan, it shall be as you wish. The Minister of the Interior will provide you with the fullest passports and authorities. *Bon voyage.*'

Thus dismissed, I bowed myself out, praying mentally that no red-tapism or bureaucracy might delay the transmission of the promised documents.

In three days I received them. The passport authorized me to travel to the end of the Czar's Asiatic dominions if I thought fit, and was worded in such a way that it obviated the necessity of obtaining a fresh passport whenever a fresh government district was to be traversed. It was not until I found the trouble, annoyance and delay I was saved by this magic strip of paper, that I fully realized how much favour had been shown me. Those few words of writing, unintelligible to me, were a magic spell, the potency of which none dared to resist.

But now, armed with power to travel, the question was, where must I go? To ascertain this, I was taken to one of the heads of the police. To him I explained my case. I described Ceneri, gave him what I supposed was about the date of his crime and trial, and begged for information as to the best means to adopt to find him in the place of his banishment.

I was most civilly treated. Indeed, for courtesy commend me to the Russian official when you are properly and powerfully accredited. Ceneri was at once identified, and his right name and secret history given to me. I recognized the name at once.

There is no need to make it public. There are many men in Europe who believe in the disinterested character and noble aims of the unfortunate convict; men who mourn him as a martyr. Perhaps in the cause of liberty he was single-hearted and noble-minded. Why should I distress his followers by revealing any dark secrets of his private life? Let him be, so far as I am concerned, Dr Ceneri to the end.

I learned from the suave, obliging Russian chief of police that a few weeks after I had seen him in Geneva, Ceneri had been arrested in St Petersburg. A deeply laid plot, involving the assassination of the Czar and several members of the government, had been revealed through the treachery of a confederate. The police, fully cognizant of everything, had waited until the pear was nearly ripe, and then struck with dire results to the plotters. Scarcely one of the principals escaped, and Ceneri, one of the most deeply implicated, was shown scant mercy. He certainly had few claims on their consideration. He was no Russian groaning under oppression and despotic government. Although he called himself Italian, he was, in truth, cosmopolitan. One of those restless spirits who wish to overturn all forms of government, save that of republican. He had plotted and schemed—even fought like a man—for Italian freedom. He had been one of Garibaldi's most trusted workmen; but had turned fiercely against his master when he found Italy was to be a kingdom, not the ideal republic of his dreams. Latterly he had directed his attention to Russia, and the plot he was engaged in having been betrayed, his career, in all human probability, was ended. After lying many months in the fortress of St Peter and St Paul, he was tried and condemned to twenty years' hard labour in Siberia. Some months ago he had been despatched to his destination, and, my informant added, was considered to have been dealt with most leniently.

Where was he now? That could not be said for certain. He might be at the Kara gold washings, at the Ustkutsk salt-works, at Troitsk, at Nertschinsk. All convicts were first sent to Tobolsk, which was a kind of general rendezvous; thence they were drafted off, at the pleasure of the Governor-General, to various places and various occupations.

If I wished, the Governor of Tobolsk should be telegraphed or written to; but, as I was bound any way to go to that town, it would be just as well if I made my inquiries in person. To this I quite agreed, mistrusting the speed of the Russian post or the newly-opened telegraph. I was ready to start tomorrow.

So, after getting all the hints and information I could, I thanked the chief for his courtesy, and with my precious papers in my pocket, went to complete my preparations for my journey; a journey which might be a thousand or two thousand miles longer or shorter, according to where it had pleased the Governor of Tobolsk to bestow the wretched Ceneri.

Before I started I received a letter from Priscilla—one of those laboured and rather misty epistles usually written by people of her station in life. It told me that Pauline was well; that she was willing to be guided by Priscilla's advice, and to remain with her until the return of her unknown relation or friend. 'But, Master Gilbert,' the letter went on, 'I am sorry to say I believe she is not quite right at times. The poor young lady talks wildly about an awful crime; but she says she is content to wait for justice to be done, as someone she has seen in her dreams during her illness is working for her. She doesn't know who it is, but it is someone who knows everything.'

This intelligence made me feel easier. Not only did it show me that Pauline would wait quietly until my return, but also that some glimmering of the immediate past might

be dawning upon her. The closing lines of Priscilla's letter
made my heart beat with hope.

'This afternoon, Master Gilbert, she seemed to discover
for the first time that she had a wedding ring on her finger.
She asked me how it came there. I told her I could not say.
Then she sat for hours and hours twisting it round and
round, thinking and thinking. I asked her, at last, what she
was thinking of. "Dreams I am trying to remember," said she,
with that pretty quiet smile of hers. I was dying to tell the dear
young lady that she was my own master's lawful wife. I was
afraid she would take the ring off, but she didn't, thank God!'

Yes, thank God, she did not! As I read Priscilla's letter I
yearned to turn homeward and fly back to my wife. But I
conquered the inclination, although I felt more and more
certain that my meeting with Ceneri would be a happy one
for me; that I should return, and, if necessary, once more place
that ring on her finger and claim her as my own, knowing
that she was purer than the gold of which that shining circlet
was made.

Pauline! my beautiful Pauline! my wife, my love, we shall
be happy yet!

The next day I started for Siberia.

CHAPTER XI

A HELL UPON EARTH

It was midsummer when I left St Petersburg. The heat was oppressive and quite disturbed my idea of the Russian climate. I went by rail to Moscow, by the iron road which runs straight as a line from the one large city to the other. The Czar ordered it to be so made, without curves or deviations. When the engineers asked him what populous places they should take on their way, his Imperial Majesty took a ruler and on the map ruled a straight line from St Petersburg to Moscow. 'Make it so,' were his commands, and so it was made, as rigid and careless of the convenience of other persons as his own despotism—a railway for some four hundred miles running simply to its destination, not daring, however much tempted, to swerve aside and disobey the autocrat's commands.

At Moscow the colossal I lingered a couple of days. It was there I had settled to engage a guide and interpreter. As I spoke two or three languages besides my own, I was able to pick and choose, and at last selected a pleasant mannered, sharp-looking young fellow who averred that he knew every inch of the great post road to the east. Then bidding farewell to the mighty Kremlin with its churches, watch-towers, and battlements, I started with my new companion for Nijnei Novgorod; at which place we must bid adieu to the railway.

We passed the old picturesque but decaying town of Vladimir, and after duly admiring its five-domed cathedral I found nothing more to distract my attention until we reached Nijnei. My companion was very anxious that we should linger for a day or two at this city. The great fair was on, and he assured me it was a sight not to be missed. I had not come to Russia to look at fairs or festivities, so commanded him to make instant preparations for continuing the journey.

We now changed our mode of conveyance. Being summer the rivers were open and navigation practicable. We took the steamer and went down the broad Volga till we passed Kasan and reached the river Kama. Up this tortuous stream we went until we landed at the large important town of Perm.

We were five days on the water—I think the five longest days I ever spent. The winding river, the slow-going steamer, made me long for the land again; there one seemed to be making progress. The road there was straight, not running into a hundred bends. We were now nearly at the end of Europe. A hundred miles further and we shall cross the Ural Mountains and be in Asiatic Russia.

At Perm we made our final preparations. From now we must depend on post-horses. Ivan, my guide, after the proper amount of haggling, bought a tarantass—a sort of phaeton. The luggage was stowed into it; we took our seats; our first relay of horses were engaged three in number and harnessed in the peculiar Russian fashion—the yemschik started them with the words of encouragement and endearment which in Russia are supposed to be more efficacious than the thong, and away we went on our long, long drive.

We crossed the Urals, which after all are not so very high. We passed the stone obelisk erected, Ivan told me, in honour of a Cossack chief named Yermak. We read the word 'Europe' on the side which first met our eyes, and turning round saw 'Asia' written on the back. I spent my first night in Asia at Ekaterineburg and lay awake the best part of it trying to calculate how many miles stretched between Pauline and myself.

For days and days have passed since I left St Petersburg, and I have travelled at all possible speed; yet the journey seems scarcely begun. Indeed, I cannot even guess at its length until I get to Tobolsk. A trifle of some four hundred miles from Ekaterineburg to Tiumen, another of two hundred from Tiumen to Tobolsk, and I shall await the pleasure of the Governor-General and what information he may choose to give me.

The carriage and ourselves are ferried across the broad yellow Irtuish—that river, the crossing of which by a Russian officer at once raises him a step in rank: for such is the inducement held out to serve in Siberia; and at the east bank of the Irtuish Siberia proper begins.

Tobolsk at last! The sight of my passports renders the Governor civility itself. He invited me to dine with him and, as for prudential reasons I thought it better to accept his invitation, treated me royally. His register told me all I wanted to know about Ceneri. He had been sent to the very extreme of the Czar's dominions, as his was a case which called for special severity. Where he would finish his journey was not settled, but that made little difference to me. As he would travel the greater part of the way on foot, and as there was but one road, I must overtake him, although he left Tobolsk months ago. The escort which accompanied that particular gang of prisoners was under the command of Captain Varlámoff, to whom his Excellency would write a few lines which I should take with me—he would also give me a supplementary passport signed by himself.

'Where do you think I shall overtake the party?' I asked.

The Governor made a calculation. 'Somewhere about Irkutsk,' he thought.

And Irkutsk two thousand miles, more or less, from Tobolsk!

I bade the great man a grateful adieu and spurred on at such speed that even the good-tempered Ivan began to grumble. Man, even a Russian, was but mortal, he said, and I could not expect to find Arab steeds among government post-horses which the postmasters were compelled to furnish at about twopence a mile a horse. I left the yemschik and himself no time for refreshment. Their tea had not grown cool enough to swallow before I was insisting on a fresh start. And as for a proper night's rest!

Tea! Until I made that journey I never knew the amount of tea a mortal stomach could hold. One and all they drank it by the gallon. They carried it about compressed into bricks, cemented, I heard with a shudder, by sheep's or some other animal's blood. They drank it morn, noon and night. Whenever there was a stoppage and boiling water could be obtained, bucketsful of tea were made and poured down their throats.

The impressions I retain of that long journey are not very deep. I was not traversing the country for the sake of writing a book of travels, or to observe the manners and customs of the people. My great object was to overtake Ceneri as quickly as possible, and my endeavours were directed to passing from one posting station to another as swiftly as I could. We sped over vast steppes, wild marshes, through forests of birch, tall pines, oak, ash, and other trees; we were ferried over broad rivers. On and on we went as straight to our destination as the great post-road would take us. When nature forced us to rest we had to put up with such pitiful accommodation as we could get. Unless the place at which we stopped was of some importance, inns were unknown. By dint of practice I at last contrived to obtain almost enough sleep, if not to satisfy me, to serve my needs, while jolting along in the tarantass.

It was a monotonous journey. I turned aside to visit no objects of interest spoken of by travellers. From morn to night, and generally through the greater part of the night, our wheels rolled along the road. And at every posting station I read on the wooden post which stands in front of it the number of miles we were from St Petersburg, until, as the days and weeks passed, I began to feel appalled at the distance I had come and the distance I must return. Should I ever see Pauline again? Who can say what may have happened before I return to England? At times I grew quite dispirited.

I think what made me realize the length of the journey even more than days or measured miles was to see, as we went on, the country people gradually changing their costume and dialect. The yemschiks who drove us changed in appearance and in nationality; the very breed of the horses varied. But let man or cattle be of what kind they may, we were well and skilfully conducted.

The weather was glorious, almost too glorious. The cultivated country we passed through looked thriving and productive. Siberia was very different in appearance from what is usually associated with its name. The air when not too warm was simply delicious. Never have I breathed a more invigorating and bracing atmosphere. There were days when the breeze seemed to send new life through every vein.

The people I thought fairly honest, and whenever I found a need of producing my papers the word civility will scarcely express the treatment I received. How I should have been treated without these potent talismans I cannot say.

The whole countryside in most places was busy with the hay harvest; a matter of such importance to the community at large that convicts are told off for some six weeks to assist in the work of saving the crops. The wild flowers, many of them very beautiful, grew freely; the people looked well and contented. Altogether my impressions of Siberia in summer were pleasant ones.

Yet I wished it had been the dead of winter. Then it is that, in spite of the cold, one travels more pleasantly. Ivan assured me that when a good snow road is formed and a tarantass may be exchanged for a sledge, the amount of ground passed over in a day is something marvellous. I am afraid from memory to say how many miles may be covered in twenty-four hours when the smooth-going runners take the place of wheels.

We had, of course, various small accidents and delays on the road. However strongly built a tarantass may be it is but mortal. Wheels broke, axletrees gave way, shafts snapped, twice we were overturned, but as no evil except delay ensued I need not relate the history of these misfortunes.

Nor need I enumerate the towns and villages through which we passed, unless l wished to make my story as interesting as a scriptural genealogy—Tara, Kainsk, Koliuvan, Tomsk, Achinsk, Krasnoyarsk, Nijnei Udinsk, may or may not be familiar to the reader, according to the depth of his geographical studies; but most of the others, even if I knew how to spell their names, would be nothing more than vain sounds. Perhaps, when we trace the march of the Russian army destined to invade our Indian Empire we may become better acquainted with the Czar's Asiatic dominions.

Yet at the entrance to each of these little towns or villages, the very names of which I have forgotten, so surely as you found the well-appointed posting station, you found also a gloomy square building, varying with the size of the place, surrounded by a tall palisade, the gates of which were barred, bolted and sentried—these buildings were the ostrogs, or prisons.

Here it was that the wretched convicts were housed as they halted on their long march. In these places they were packed like sardines in a box. Prisons built to hold two hundred were often called upon to accommodate at least twice that number of luckless wretches. I was told that when ice was breaking up in the rivers; when the floods were out; when in fact the progress must perforce be delayed, the scenes at these prisons or depots beggared description. Men, sometimes unsexed women with them, huddled into rooms reeking with filth, the floors throwing out poisonous emanations—rooms built to give but scanty space to a small number, crowded to suffocation. The mortality at times was fearful. The trials of the march were as nothing when compared to the horrors of the so-called rest. And it was in one of these ostrogs I should find Ceneri.

We passed many gangs of convicts plodding along to their fate. Ivan told me that most of them were in chains. This I should not have noticed, as the irons are only on the legs and worn under the trousers. Poor wretched beings, my heart ached for them! Felons though they were, I could never refuse the charity they invariably prayed for. So far as I could see they were not unkindly treated by the soldiers and officers, but terrible tales were told me about their sufferings at the hands of inhuman gaolers and commandants of prisons. There, for the slightest infraction of the rules, the rod, the dark cell, and a variety of other punishments were called into play.

I always felt relieved when we had passed out of sight of a gang like this. The contrast between my own position and that of such a number of my fellow-men was too painful to contemplate—and yet if Ceneri did not clear away every shadow of doubt from my mind I might retrace my steps a more miserable wretch than either of those foot-sore convicts

Some week or ten days after leaving Tobolsk I began to make inquiries at every ostrog as to when Captain Varlámoff's gang passed, and when I might expect to overtake it. The answers I received to the latter question corresponded with that given me by the Governor—all agreed at Irkutsk, or just beyond. Day after day I found we were gaining rapidly upon the party, and when at last we reached the large handsome town of Irkutsk I rightly reckoned that I had reached the end, or nearly the end of my journey.

On inquiry I found Captain Varlámoff had not yet arrived. At the place where I had last inquired I had been told he had passed through a day before, so it was evident we had overlooked and outstripped them. The best thing to be done was to wait in Irkutsk the arrival of the party.

I was not at all sorry to take a couple of days' rest after my fatigues. I was not sorry to indulge once more in the comforts of comparative civilization; yet nearly every hour I was sending down to inquire if the convicts had arrived. More ardently than I had longed to reach Irkutsk, I longed to turn the horses' heads westward and start on the return journey.

I had heard no news from home since I left St Petersburg. Indeed, I could not expect a letter, as after my departure from Nijnei Novgorod, I had positively outstripped the post. On the road home I hoped to find letters waiting me.

After I had kicked my heels in Irkutsk for two days I received the welcome news that Captain Varlámoff had marched his prisoners to the ostrog at four o'clock that afternoon. I rose from my dinner and went with all speed to the prison.

A man in plain clothes—a civilian—demanding to be conducted to the presence of a Russian captain who had just arrived from a long march, seemed almost too great a joke for the sentries to bear in a soldierlike manner. Their stolid faces broke into scornful smiles as they asked Ivan if 'the little father' had quite gone mad. It required much firmness, much persuasion and a gratuity, which to the simple military mind represented an unlimited quantity of 'vodka', and consequently many happy drinking bouts, before I was allowed to pass through the gates of the high palisade, and, with many misgivings on the part of my guide, was conducted to the presence of the Captain.

A fine fierce-looking young soldier, who glared at me for disturbing him; for having, by advice, adopted the Russian costume, which by now was stained and frayed by travel, there was nothing to show him I was not a civilian whom any soldier might kick at his pleasure.

It was delightful to see the change the perusal of the Tobolsk governor's letter made in the Captain's appearance. He rose, and with the greatest courtesy offered me a chair, and asked me in French if I spoke that language.

I assured him on that point, and finding I could dispense with Ivan's services, sent him outside to wait for me.

Varlámoff would not hear of commencing business until wine and cigarettes made their appearance—then he was at my service in anything and everything.

I told him what I desired.

'To speak in private with one of my convicts. Certainly—this letter places me at your commands. But which convict?'

I gave him the true name. He shook his head.

'I know none of them by that name. Most of the names the political prisoners pass under are false ones. When they leave me they will become numbers, so it doesn't matter.'

I suggested Ceneri. He shook his head again.

'I know the man I want is with you,' I said. 'How shall I find him?'

'You know him by sight?'

'Yes—well.'

'Then you had better come with me and try and pick him out among my unfortunates. Light another cigarette—you will want it,' he added, with meaning.

He led the way, and soon we stood before a heavy door. At his command a gaoler, armed with mighty keys, appeared. The grinding locks were turned, and the door was opened.

'Follow me,' said Varlámoff, with a long pull at his cigarette. I obeyed, and standing on the threshold had much ado to keep from fainting.

From the stench which rushed through it, that open door might have been the entrance to some pestilential cavern at the bottom of which all the impurities of the world were rotting and putrefying. As it passed you, you felt that the thick air was poisonous with disease and death.

I recovered myself as best I could, and followed my guide into the grim interior. The door closed behind us.

Had I the power to describe the sights I saw when my eyes grew accustomed to the gloom, I should not be believed. The prison was spacious, but when the number of the prisoners was considered, it should have been three times the size. It was thronged with wretched beings. They were standing, sitting and lying about. Men of all ages and, it seemed, of all nationalities. Men with features of the lowest human type. They were huddled in groups—many were quarrelling, cursing and swearing. Moved by curiosity they pressed around us as closely as they dared, laughing and jabbering in their barbarous dialects. I was in a hell, an obscene, unclean hell! a hell made by men for their fellow-men.

Filth! the place was one mass of it. Filth under foot—filth on the walls, the rafters and the beams—filth floating about in the hot, heavy, pestiferous air. Each man seemed to be a moving mass of filth. Zola would revel in a minute description of the horrors of that place, but I must leave them to the imagination, although I know and even trust that no one's imagination can come near the reality.

The only thing I could think of was this. Why did not these men rush out, overpower the guards, and escape from this reeking den? I put the question to Varlámoff.

'They never attempt to escape whilst on the march,' he said. 'It is a point of honour among them. If one escapes those left are treated with much greater severity.'

'Do none ever get away?'

'Yes, many do when they are sent to the works. But it does them no good. They must pass through the towns on their flight or they would starve. Then they are always caught and sent back.'

I was peering into all the faces about, trying to find the one I sought. My inspection was received with looks sullen, suspicious, defiant or careless. Remarks were made in undertones, but Varlámoff's dreaded presence kept me from insult. I examined many groups without success, then I made a tour of the prison.

All along the wall was a slanting platform upon which men lay in various attitudes. Being the most comfortable station, every inch of it was covered by recumbent forms. In the angle formed by the prison walls I saw a man reclining, as if utterly worn out. His head sank down upon his breast, his eyes were closed. There was something in his figure which struck me as familiar. I walked to him and laid my hand upon his shoulder. He opened his weary eyes and raised his sad face. It was Manuel Ceneri!

CHAPTER XII

THE NAME OF THE MAN

HE looked at me with an expression in his eyes which passed at once from hopelessness to bewilderment. He seemed to be uncertain whether it was a phantom or a man he was looking at. He rose to his feet in a dazed, stupefied way, and stood face to face with me, whilst his wretched fellow-prisoners pressed curiously around us.

'Mr Vaughan! Here! In Siberia!' he said, as one not believing his own senses.

'I have come from England to see you. This is the prisoner I am looking for,' I said, turning to the officer who stood at my side, mitigating to some extent the noxiousness of the atmosphere by the cigarette he puffed vigorously.

'I am glad you have found him,' he said, politely. 'Now the sooner we get outside the better, the air here is unhealthy.'

Unhealthy! It was fetid! I was filled with wonder, as I looked at the bland French-speaking Captain at my side, at the state of mind to which a man must bring himself before he could calmly stand in the midst of his fellow-creatures and see such misery unconcernedly—could even think he was but doing his duty. Perhaps he was. It may be the crimes of the prisoners forbade sympathy. But, oh! to stand there in the midst of those poor wretches, turned for the time into little more than animals! I may be wrong but it seems to me that the gaoler must have a harder heart than the worst of his captives!

'I can see him—talk to him alone?' I asked

'Certainly; so you are authorized to do. I am a soldier; you in this matter are my superior officer.'

'May I take him to the inn?'

124

'I think not. I will find you a room here. Please follow me. Phew! that is a relief.'

We were now outside the prison door and breathing fresh air once more. The Captain led me to a kind of office, dirty and furnished barely enough, but a paradise compared to the scene we had just quitted.

'Wait here; I will send the prisoner to you.'

As he turned to leave me I thought of the miserable, dejected appearance Ceneri had presented. Let him be the greatest villain in the world, I could not keep from wishing to do some little thing to benefit him.

'I may give him food and drink?' I asked.

The Captain shrugged his shoulders and laughed good temperedly.

'He ought not to be hungry. He has the rations which government says are sufficient. But then you may be hungry and thirsty. If so, I do not see how I can stop you sending for wine and food—of course for yourself.'

I thanked him and forthwith despatched my guide in quest of the best wine and meat he could get. Wine, when ordered by a gentleman, means in Russia but one thing—champagne. At an inn of any standing, champagne, or at least its substitute, wine of the Don, may be procured. My messenger soon returned with a bottle of the real beverage and a good supply of cold meat and white bread. As soon as it was placed on the rough table a tall soldier led in my expected guest

I placed a chair for Ceneri, into which he sank wearily. As he did so I heard the jingle of the irons on his legs. Then I told my interpreter to leave us. The soldier, who no doubt had received his orders, saluted me gravely and followed his example. The door closed behind him, and Ceneri and I were alone.

He had somewhat recovered from his stupefaction, and as he looked at me I saw an eager, wistful expression on his face. Drowning as he was, no doubt he caught at the straw of my unexpected appearance, thinking it might assist him to freedom. Perhaps it was to enjoy a moment or two brightened by the faintest or wildest gleam of hope that made him pause before he spoke to me.

'I have come a long, long way to see you, Dr Ceneri,' I began.

'If the way seemed long to you, what has it been to me? You at least can return when you like to freedom and happiness.'

He spoke in the quiet tone of despair. I had been unable to prevent my words sounding cold and my voice being stern. If my coming had raised any hope in his heart, my manner now dispelled it. He knew I had not made the journey for his sake.

'Whether I can go back to happiness or not depends on what you tell me. You may imagine it is no light matter which has brought me so far to see you for a few minutes.'

He looked at me curiously, but not suspiciously. I could do him no harm—for him the outer world was at an end. If I accused him of fifty murders, and brought each one home to him, his fate could be no worse. He was blotted out, erased; nothing now could matter to him, except more or less bodily discomfort. I shuddered as l realized what his sentence meant, and in spite of myself, a compassionate feeling stole over me.

'I have much of importance to say, but first let me give you some wine and food.'

'Thank you,' he said, almost humbly. 'You would scarcely believe, Mr Vaughan, that a man may be reduced to such a state that he can hardly restrain himself at the sight of decent meat and drink.'

I could believe anything after the interior of the ostrog. I opened the wine and placed it before him. As he ate and drank, I had leisure to observe him attentively.

His sufferings had wrought a great change in him. Every feature vas sharpened, every limb seemed slighter—he looked at least ten years older. He wore the Russian peasants' ordinary garments, and these hung in rags about him. His feet, swathed in fragments of some woollen material, showed in places through his boots. The long, weary marches were telling their tale upon his frame. He had never given me the idea of being a robust man, and as I looked at him I thought that whatever work he might be put to, it would not pay the Russian Government for his sorry keep. But the probabilities were, they would not have to keep him long.

He ate not voraciously, but with a keen appetite. The wine he used sparingly. His meal being finished, he glanced around as if in quest of something. I guessed what he wanted and passed him my cigar-case and a light. He thanked me and began to smoke with an air of enjoyment.

For a while I had not the heart to interrupt the poor wretch. When he left me it must be to return to that hell peopled by human beings. But time was slipping by. Outside the door I could hear the monotonous step of the sentry, and I did not know what period of grace the polite Captain might allow to his prisoner.

Ceneri was leaning back in his chair with a kind of dreamy look on his face, smoking slowly and placidly, taking, as it were, everything he could out of the luxury of a good cigar. I asked him to drink some more wine. He shook his head, then turned and looked at me.

'Mr Vaughan,' he said; 'yes, it is Mr Vaughan. But who and what am I? Where are we? Is it London, Geneva, or elsewhere? Shall I awake and find I have dreamed of what I have suffered?'

'I am afraid it is no dream. We are in Siberia.'

'And you are not come to bear me good news? You are not one of us—a friend trying at the peril of your life to set me free?'

I shook my head. 'I would do all I could to make your lot easier, but I come with a selfish motive to ask some questions which you alone can answer.'

'Ask them. You have given me an hour's relief from misery; I am grateful.'

'You will answer truly?'

'Why not? I have nothing to fear, nothing to gain, nothing to hope. Falsehood is forced on people by circumstances; a man in my state has no need of it.'

'The first question I have to ask is—who and what is that man Macari?'

Ceneri sprang to his feet. The name of Macari seemed to bring him back to the world. He looked no longer a decrepit man. His voice was fierce and stern.

'A traitor! a traitor!' he cried. 'But for him I should have succeeded and escaped. If he were only standing in your place! Weak as I am, I could find strength enough to cling on to his throat till the vile breath was out of his accursed body!'

He walked up and down the room, clenching and unclenching his hands.

'Try and be calm, Dr Ceneri,' I said. 'I have nothing to do with his plots and political treasons. Who is he? What is his parentage? Is Macari his name?'

'The only name I ever knew him by. His father was a renegade Italian who sent his son to live in England for fear his precious blood should be spilt in freeing his country. I found him a young man and made him one of us. His perfect knowledge of your tongue was of great service; and he fought—yes, once he fought like a man. Why did he turn traitor now? Why do you ask these questions?'

'He has been to me and asserts that he is Pauline's brother.'

Ceneri's face, as he heard this intelligence, was enough to banish lie number one from my mind. My heart leapt as I guessed that number two would be disposed of as easily. But there was a terrible revelation to be made when I came to ask about that.

'Pauline's brother!' stammered Ceneri. 'Her brother! She has none.'

A sickly look crept over his features as he spoke—a look the meaning of which I could not read.

'He says he is Anthony March, her brother.'

'Anthony March!' gasped Ceneri 'There is no such person. What did he want—his object?' he continued feverishly.

'That I should join him in a memorial to the Italian Government, asking for a return of some portion of the fortune you spent.'

Ceneri laughed a bitter laugh. 'All grows clear,' he said. 'He betrayed a plot which might have changed a government for the sake of getting me out of the way. Coward! Why not have killed me and only me? Why have made others suffer with me? Anthony March! My God! that man is a villain!'

'You are sure that Macari betrayed you?'

'Sure! yes. I was sure when the man in the cell next to mine rapped it on the wall. He had means of knowing.'

'I don't understand you.'

'Prisoners can sometimes talk to each other by taps on the wall which divides their cells. The man next to me was one of us. Long before he went raving mad from the months of solitary confinement, he rapped out, over and over again, "Betrayed by Macari." I believed him. He was too true a man to make the accusation without proof. But until now I could not see the object of the treason.'

The easiest part of my task was over. Macari's assumed relationship to Pauline was disposed of. Now if Ceneri would tell me, I must learn who was the victim of that crime committed years ago, and what was the reason for the foul deed. I must learn that Macari's explanation was an utter falsehood, prompted by malice, or else my journey would have benefited me nothing. Is it any wonder that my lips trembled as I endeavoured to approach the subject?

'Now, Dr Ceneri,' I said, 'I have a question of weightier import to ask. Had Pauline a lover before I married her?'

He raised his eyebrows. 'Surely you have not come here to ask that question—to have a fit of jealousy cured?'

'No,' I said; 'you will hear my meaning later on. Meanwhile, answer me.'

'She had a lover, for Macari professed to love her, and swore she should be his wife. But I can most certainly say she never returned his love.'

'Nor loved anyone else?'

'Not to my knowledge. But your manner, your words are strange. Why do you ask? I may have wronged you, Mr Vaughan, but save for the one thing, her mind, Pauline was fit to be your wife.'

'You did wrong me—you know it. What right had you to let me marry a woman whose senses were disarranged? It was cruel to both.'

I felt stern and spoke sternly. Ceneri shifted in his chair uneasily. If I had wished revenge it was here. Gazing on this wretched, ragged, broken-down man, and knowing what awaited him when he left me, would have filled the measure desired by the most vengeful heart.

I wanted no revenge on the man. His manner told me he spoke the truth when he denied that Pauline had ever been in love. As, when last I gazed on her fair face, I knew it would, Macari's black lie had been scouted. Pauline was innocent as an angel. But I must know who was the man whose death had for a while deprived her of reason.

Ceneri was glancing at me nervously. Did he guess what I had to ask him? 'Tell me,' I said, 'the name of the young man murdered by Macari in London, in the presence of Pauline; tell me why he was killed.'

His face grew ashen. He seemed to collapse—to sink back into his chair a helpless heap, without the power of speech or movement, without the power of turning his eyes from my face.

'Tell me—' I repeated. 'Stay, I will recall the scene to you, and you will know I am well informed. Here is the table; here is Macari, standing over the man he has stabbed; here are you, and behind you is another man with a scar on his cheek. In the back room, at the piano, is Pauline. She is singing, but her song stops as the murdered man falls dead. Do I describe the scene truly?'

I had spoken excitedly. I had used gestures and words. Ceneri's ears had drunk in every syllable; his eyes had followed every gesture. As I pointed to the supposed position of Pauline, he had looked there with a quick, startled glance, as if expecting to see her enter the door. He made no attempt to deny the accuracy of my representation.

I waited for him to recover. He was looking ghastly. His breath came in spasmodic gasps. For a moment I feared he was about to die then and there. I poured out a glass of wine; he took it in his trembling hand and gulped it down.

'Tell me his name.' I repeated. 'Tell me what he had to do with Pauline.'

Then he found his voice. 'Why do you come here to ask me? Pauline could have told you. She must be well, or you could not have learned this.'

'She has told me nothing.'

'You are wrong. She must have told you. No one else saw the crime—the murder: for a murder it was.'

'There was another present besides the actors I have named.'

Ceneri started and looked at me.

'Yes, there was another; there by an accident. A man who could hear but not see. A man whose life I pleaded for as for my own.'

'I thank you for having saved it.'

'*You* thank me. Why should *you* thank me?'

'If you saved anyone's life it was mine. I was that man.'

'You that man?' He looked at me more attentively. 'Yes: now the features come back to me. I always wondered that your face seemed so familiar. Yes. I can understand—I am a doctor—your eyes were operated upon?'

'Yes—most successfully.'

'You can see well now—but then! I could not be mistaken, you were blind—you saw nothing.'

'I saw nothing, but I heard everything.'

'And now Pauline has told you what happened?'

'Pauline has not spoken.'

Ceneri rose, and in great agitation walked up and down the room, his chains rattling as he moved.

'I knew it,' he muttered, in Italian, 'I knew it—such a crime cannot be hidden.'

Then be turned to me. 'Tell me how you have learned this? Teresa would die before she spoke. Petróff is dead—died, as I told you, raving mad.'

From his last words I presumed that Petróff was the third man I had seen, and also the fellow-prisoner who had denounced Macari.

'Was it Macari—that double-dyed traitor? No—he was the murderer—such an avowal would defeat his ends. Tell me how you know!'

'I would tell you, but I suspect you would not believe me.'

'Believe you?' he cried, excitedly. 'I would believe anything connected with that night—it has never left my thoughts—Mr Vaughan, the truth has come to me in my captivity. I am not condemned to this life for a political crime. My sentence is God's indirect vengeance for the deed you witnessed.'

It was clear that Ceneri was not such a hardened human as Macari. He, at least, had a conscience. Moreover, as he appeared to be superstitious, he would perhaps believe me when I told him how my accurate knowledge had been obtained.

'I will tell you,' I said, 'provided you pledge your honour to give me the full history of that fearful crime and answer my questions fully and truthfully.'

He smiled bitterly. 'You forget my position, Mr Vaughan, when you speak of "honour". Yet I promise all you ask.'

So I told him, as shortly and simply as I could, all that had occurred; all I had seen. He shuddered as I again described the terrible vision.

'Spare me,' he said, 'I know it all. Thousands of times I have seen it or have dreamed it—it will never leave me. But why come to me? Pauline, you say, is recovering her senses—she would have told you all.'

'I would not ask her until I saw you. She is herself again, but I am a stranger to her—and unless your answer is the one I hope for, we shall never meet again.'

'If anything I can do to atone—' he began, eagerly.

'You can only speak the truth. Listen. I taxed the murderer, your accomplice, with the crime. Like you he could not deny it, but he justified it.'

'How?—tell me,' panted Ceneri.

For a moment I paused. I fixed my eyes upon him to catch every change of feature—to read the truth in more than words.

'He vowed to me that the young man was killed by your instructions—that he was—oh God, how can I repeat it?—the lover of Pauline, who having dishonoured her, refused to repair his fault. The truth! Tell me the truth!'

I almost shouted the last words—my calmness vanished as I thought of the villain who had, with a mocking smile, coupled Pauline's name with shame.

Ceneri, on the other hand, grew calmer as he grasped the purport of my question. Bad as the man might be, even stained with innocent blood, I could have clasped him in my arms as I read in his wondering eyes the baselessness of the foul accusation.

'That young man—the boy struck down by Macari's dagger—was Pauline's brother—my sister's son—Anthony March!'

CHAPTER XIII

A TERRIBLE CONFESSION

CENERI, having made this astounding announcement, threw his wasted arms across the rough table and laid his head upon them with a gesture of despair. I sat like one stupefied, repeating mechanically, 'Pauline's brother—Anthony March!' Every vestige of the black lie was swept away from my mind; but the crime in which Ceneri had been concerned assumed more fearful proportions. It was more dreadful than I had suspected. The victim a near blood relation—his own sister's child! Nothing, I felt, could be urged to excuse or palliate the crime. Even had he not ordered and planned it, he had been present; had assisted in hiding all traces of it; had been, until recently, on terms of friendship with the man who had struck the blow. I could scarcely control the loathing and contempt I felt for the abject wretch before me. My burning indignation would scarcely allow me to ask him, in intelligible speech, the object of the cruel deed. But for once and all I must have everything made clear to me.

I was spared the necessity of asking the question I was trying to force to my lips. The convict raised his head and looked at me with miserable eyes.

'You shrink from me. No wonder. Yet I am not so guilty as you think.'

'Tell me all, first; the excuses may come afterward, if anything can be urged in excuse of the crime.'

I spoke as I felt—sternly and contemptuously.

'None can be urged for the murder. For me, God knows I would willingly have let that bright boy live. He forsook and forgot his country, but that I forgave.'

'His country! his father's country was England!'

'His mother's was Italy,' replied Ceneri, almost fiercely. 'He had our blood in his veins. His mother was a true Italian. She would have given fortune, life—aye, even honour, for Italy.'

'No matter. Tell me the whole terrible story.'

He told me. In justice to a penitent man, I do not use his own words in re-telling it. Without his accent and stress they would sound cold and unemotional. Criminal he had been, but not so utterly black as my fancy had painted him. His great fault was that in the cause of liberty any weapons were allowable, any crimes were pardonable. We Englishmen, whose idea of tyranny and oppression is being debarred from the exercise of the franchise, can neither understand nor sympathize with a man of his type. We may call the government righteous or corrupt as we are Whigs or Tories, and one side happens to be in or out; but, at least, we are ruled by our countrymen, elected by some of us for that purpose. Let us be for years and years at the mercy of a foreigner, and we may understand what patriotism in Ceneri's sense means.

He and his sister were the children of respectable middle-class people—not noble as Macari asserted. He had been given a liberal education, and adopted the profession of a doctor. His sister, from whom Pauline inherited her great beauty, lived the life of an ordinary Italian girl—a duller life, perhaps, than many of them led, as, following her brother's example, she refused to share in gaieties whilst the white-coated foe ruled the land. No doubt she would have been faithful to her mourning for her country had not love come upon the scene. An Englishman named March saw the fair Italian girl, won her heart, wedded her and carried her away in triumph to his native land. Ceneri never quite forgave his sister for her desertion and defection; but the prospects opened before her by the marriage were so great that he made little opposition to it. March was a very rich man. He was the only son of an only son, which fact accounts for

Pauline having, so far as Ceneri knew, no near relatives on her father's side. For several years the young husband and his beautiful dark-eyed wife lived in great happiness. Two children, a son and a daughter, were born to them. When the son was twelve and the daughter ten years old the father died. The widow, who had made few close friends in England, and only loved the country for her husband's sake, flew back to her native land. She was cordially welcomed by her old friends. She was considered fabulously wealthy. Her husband, in the first flush of his passion, had made a will bequeathing everything he possessed to her absolutely. Although children had since come, so perfectly did he trust her that no change had been made as to the disposition of his property. So, with such a fortune at her command, Mrs March was honoured and courted by all.

She had, until she met her future husband, loved her brother above everyone in the world. She had echoed his patriotism, sympathized with him in his schemes and listened to the wild plots he was always planning He was some years older than she was, and upon her return to Italy she found him, outwardly, nothing more than a quiet, hard-working, ill-paid doctor. She marvelled at the change from the headstrong, visionary, daring young man she had left. It was not until he was certain her heart had not forsaken her country that Ceneri allowed her to see that under his prosaic exterior lurked one of the subtlest and ablest minds of all those engaged in working out the liberation of Italy. Then all his old sway came back. She admired, almost worshipped him. She, too, was ready to make any sacrifice when the time should come.

What she would have done had she been called upon it is impossible to say; but there is little doubt but her fortune and her children's fortune would have been freely spent in the good cause. As it was, she died long before the pear was ripe, and when she died, such was her faith in her brother, everything was left in his hands as sole trustee for her children.

In her last moments the thought of her husband's decided English proclivities made her exact a promise that both the boy and the girl should be given an English education. Then she closed her eyes, and the orphans were left entirely to the trustee's mercy.

He obeyed her spoken commands to the letter. Anthony and Pauline were sent to English schools; but having no friends in their father's native land, or all old friends having been lost sight of during their mother's widowhood, the holidays were spent in Italy. They grew up almost as much Italian as English. Ceneri husbanded, invested, and managed their fortune with care and in a businesslike way. I have no doubt, so far as it went, his honesty was unimpeachable.

Then the longed-for moment came! The great blow was to be struck. Ceneri, who had kept himself out of little abortive plots, felt that now or never he must do all he could do for his country. He hailed the coming man. He knew that Garibaldi was to be the saviour of his oppressed land. The first rash step had been taken and led to success. The time and the man were at hand. Recruits were flocking by thousands to the scene of war, but the cry was 'Money, money, money!' Money for arms and ammunition—money for stores, food and clothing—money for bribes—money for everything! Those who furnished the sinews of war would be the real liberators of their country!

Why should he hesitate? Had his sister lived she would have given all the fortune she possessed as freely as she would have given her life! Were not her children half Italian? Liberty laughed at such a small thing as breach of trust.

Except a few thousand pounds, he ruthlessly realized and sacrificed the whole of the children's inheritance. He poured their thousands and thousands into the hands held out for them. The large sum was spent where it was most wanted, and Ceneri averred that he freed Italy by the opportune aid. Perhaps he did—who can tell?

Titles and honours were afterwards offered him for this great though secret service. It makes me think better of the man that he refused all reward. His conscience may have told him he had not robbed himself. Anyway, he remained plain Doctor Ceneri, and broke with his old leaders and friends when he found that Italy was to be a kingdom, not a republic.

He had kept, I said, a few thousand pounds. The boy and the girl were growing up, and their uncle thought that even his patriotism permitted him to keep back enough to complete their education and start them in life. Pauline was promising to be so beautiful that he troubled little about her future. A rich husband would set everything right with her. But Anthony—who was becoming a wild, headstrong young fellow—was another affair.

As soon as the youth should reach man's estate, Ceneri had resolved to make a clean breast of his defalcations—to tell him how the money had been spent—to beg his forgiveness, and, if necessary, bear the penalty of his fraudulent act. But so long as any money remained he delayed doing so. The young man, if evincing no sympathy with his uncle's regeneration schemes and pursuit of liberty, fully believed in his integrity. Feeling assured that when he came of age he would succeed to a splendid inheritance, swelled by accumulated savings, he threw away money in a thousand and one extravagant ways, till Ceneri soon saw that the end of the reserve fund was drawing near.

So long as he had the money in hand to meet Anthony's demands, he postponed the evil day of confession. The idea, which Macari had tried to work out with my aid, of appealing to the Italian Government for a return of some of the amounts expended, suggested itself to him; but to carry this out it would be necessary to let his nephew know what had taken place—the appeal must be made in his name.

As the inevitable exposure drew near he dreaded it more and more. He had studied Anthony's character, and felt sure that when he knew the truth his one wish would be to take revenge on the fraudulent trustee. Ceneri could see nothing before him but a well-deserved term of penal servitude. If the English law failed to touch him, that of his own country might be brought against him.

It seems to me that until this time he had committed no crime from which he could not absolve himself on the grounds of patriotism; but now the desire to save himself from punishment grew upon him, and he determined to avoid the consequences of his acts.

He had never felt any great affection for the two children. No doubt they had latterly appeared in the light of wronged innocents who would one day demand a reckoning with him. They were in disposition too much like their father for him to be greatly drawn toward them. He despised Anthony for his gay, frivolous life—a life without plans or ambition—and contrasted it with his own. He honestly believed he was doing good work in the world; that his plots and conspiracies quickened the steps of universal liberty. In his dark, secret circle, he was a figure of considerable importance. If he were ruined and imprisoned he would be missed. Had he not a right to weigh his own high purposes against the butterfly existence of his nephew?

So he reasoned and persuaded himself that, for the sake of mankind, he might do almost anything to save himself.

Anthony March was now twenty-two. Trusting his uncle; careless and easy going; so long as his wants had been supplied he had accepted, until now, the excuses made for deferring the settlement of his affairs. Whether his suspicions had at last been awakened or not cannot be said; but recently he had taken another tone, and was insisting that his fortune should be at once placed in his hands. Ceneri, whose schemes called him for a time to England, pacified him by assuring that he would, during his stay in London, explain everything.

The explanation must indeed be given now, as Anthony's last drafts had reduced the remnant of his father's wealth almost to nothing.

Now, as to Macari's part in the affair. He had been for years a useful and trusted agent of Ceneri's; but most probably without the latter's lofty and unselfish aims. He appears to have followed conspiracy as a trade by which money might be made. The fact, which seems beyond a doubt, that he fought bravely and distinguished himself on the battlefield, may be accounted for by the natural ferocity of the man's nature, which bade him fight for the sake of fighting.

Being mixed up in all his plots he was often at Ceneri's house, wherever for the time being it might be; and on many occasions saw Pauline. He fell in love with her when she was but a young girl, and tried everything he knew to win her heart. To her he was soft and kind. She had no reason to mistrust him, but she utterly refused to give him the love he asked for. The pursuit went on at intervals for years—the man, to give him his due, was constancy itself. Again and again Pauline assured him of the hopelessness of his suit, but after each rebuff he returned to the attack.

Ceneri gave him no encouragement. He did not wish to offend him, and seeing that the girl was proof against his blandishments, let things alone, hoping that Macari would grow weary of urging those requests which were always met by refusals. He believed that he was not seeking Pauline for the sake of the money which should have been hers. Macari knew what large sums Ceneri had poured into the patriot's treasury, and, no doubt guessed whence they came.

Pauline remained at school until she was nearly eighteen; then she spent two years with her uncle in Italy. It was a dull life for the girl, and she sighed audibly for England. Although meeting him seldom, she was passionately attached to her brother, and was greatly delighted when Ceneri told her that business would take him for a while to London, and that she might accompany him. She was growing tired of Macari's pertinacity, and, moreover, longed to see her brother again.

Ceneri, for the sake of receiving his many political friends at what hours of the day or night he chose, took a furnished house for a short term. Pauline's disgust was great when she found that one of their first visitors was Macari. His presence was so indispensable to Ceneri that he took up his abode with them in Horace Street. As old Teresa, the doctor's servant, accompanied the party and waited upon them, the change to Pauline was a very slight one.

Macari still persecuted the girl without success. At last, almost desperate, he formed the wild plan of trying to enlist her brother on his side His idea was that Pauline's love for Anthony would induce her to yield to any wish he expressed He was no particular friend of the young man's, but, having once rendered him a signal service, felt himself entitled to ask a favour at his hands. Knowing that both brother and sister were penniless, he had less hesitation in so doing.

He called on Anthony and made his request. Anthony, who seems to have been a proud, arrogant and not a very pleasant young man, simply laughed at his impertinence and bade him begone. Poor boy, he little knew what that laugh would cost him!

It may have been the retort made by Macari, as he departed in a whirlwind of rage, that opened Anthony's eyes as to the jeopardy in which his fortune was placed. Anyway he wrote at once to his uncle, insisting upon an immediate settlement. In the event of any delay he would consult a solicitor, and if necessary take criminal proceedings against the trustee.

The moment which Ceneri had so long dreaded—so long postponed—had come; only now, the confession, instead of being as he intended a voluntary one, would be wrung from him.

Whether he would be amenable to the Italian or English law he did not know, but he felt certain that Anthony would at once take steps to ensure his arrest and detention. The latter, if only temporary, would ruin the scheme upon which he was now engaged. At any cost Anthony March must be silenced for a time.

He assured me with the solemnity of a dying man that no thought of the dreadful means which effected this was in his mind. He had revolved many plans and finally settled on one which, although difficult to execute and very hazardous, seemed to give the best promise of success. His intention was, with the assistance of his friends and subordinates, to carry Anthony abroad and deposit him for some months in a lunatic asylum. The confinement was only to be temporary; yet although Ceneri did not confess to it, I have little doubt but the young man would have been asked to buy his freedom by a promise to forgive the misappropriation of the trust money.

And now as to carrying this precious plan into execution. Macari, vowing vengeance for the words of insult, was ready to aid in every way. Petróff, the man with the scarred face, was the doctor's, body and soul. Teresa, the old servant, would have committed any crime at her master's command. The necessary papers could be obtained or forged. Let the conspirators get Anthony to visit them at the house in Horace Street and he should leave it only as a lunatic in charge of his doctor and his keepers. It was a vile, treacherous scheme, the success of which was very doubtful, necessitating, as it must, carrying the victim to Italy. How this was to be done Ceneri did not exactly explain—perhaps he had not quite worked out the details of the plot—perhaps the boy was to be drugged—perhaps he counted upon his frantic state when he discovered the true position of affairs to give colour to the statement that he was of unsound mind.

The first thing was to induce Anthony to come to Horace Street at an hour suitable for development of the plot. Ceneri made his preparations; gave his instructions to his confederates, and then wrote to his nephew begging him to call upon him that night and hear his explanation of matters.

Perhaps Anthony mistrusted his relative and his associates more than was suspected. Anyway, he replied by declining the invitation, but suggested that his uncle should call upon him instead. Then, by Macari's advice. Pauline was made the innocent means of luring her brother to the fatal house. Ceneri expressed his perfect indifference as to where the meeting took place, but, being very much engaged, postponed it for a day or two. He then told Pauline that as business would keep him from home until late the next night, it would be a good opportunity for her to spend some time with her brother—she had better ask him to come and see her during his absence. As he also wished to see Anthony, she must endeavour to keep him until his return.

Pauline, suspecting nothing, wrote to her brother, and, saying she would be all alone until late at night, begged him to come to her, or, if he would, take her to some place of amusement. They went to the theatre together, and it was twelve o'clock before he brought her back to Horace Street. No doubt she begged him to remain with her awhile—perhaps against his will. Awful as the shock of what followed was to the girl, it must have been doubly so when she knew that her entreaties had led him to his death.

The brother and sister sat alone for some time; then Ceneri and his two friends made their appearance. Anthony seemed displeased at the encounter, but made the best of matters and greeted his uncle civilly. Macari he simply turned his back upon.

It was no part of Ceneri's plan that any act of violence or restraint should take place in the presence of Pauline. Whatever was to be done should be done when Anthony was about to leave the house. Then he might be seized and conveyed to the cellar: his cries if needful being stifled. Pauline was to know nothing about it. Arrangements had been made for her to go on the morrow to a friend of her uncle's, with whom she was to stay, ignorant of the purport of the business which suddenly called the plotters away.

'Pauline,' said Ceneri, 'I think you had better go to bed. Anthony and I have some affairs to speak about.'

'I will wait until Anthony leaves,' she said, 'but if you want to talk I will go into the other room.'

So saying, she passed through the folding doors and went to the piano, where she sat playing and singing for her own amusement.

'It is too late to talk about business tonight,' said Anthony, as his sister left the room.

'You had better take this opportunity. I find I must leave England tomorrow.'

Anthony, having no wish to let his uncle escape without an explanation, reseated himself.

'Very well,' he said; 'but there is no need to have strangers present.'

'They are scarcely strangers. They are friends of mine, who will vouch for the truth of what I am going to say.'

'I will not have my affairs talked about before a man like that,' said Anthony, with a motion of contempt toward Macari.

The two men were conversing in a low tone. Pauline was not far off, and neither wished to alarm her by high words or by the appearance of a pending quarrel; but Macari heard the remark and saw the gesture. His eyes blazed and he leaned forward toward young March.

'It may be, in a few days,' he said, 'you will be willing enough to give me freely the gift you refused a short time ago.'

Ceneri noticed that the speaker's right hand was inside the breast of his coat, but this being a favourite attitude of his, thought nothing of it.

Anthony did not condescend to reply. He turned from the man with a look of utter contempt—a look which, no doubt, drove Macari almost beside himself with rage.

'Before we talk about anything else,' he said to his uncle, 'I shall insist that from now Pauline is placed under my care. Neither she nor her fortune shall become the prey of a low-bred, beggarly Italian adventurer like this man, your friend.'

These were the last words the poor boy ever spoke. Macari took one step toward him—he made no exclamation of rage—hissed out no oath which might warn his victim. Grasped in his right hand, the long bright steel leapt from its lurking place, and as Anthony March looked up, and then threw himself back in his chair to avoid him, the blow was struck downward with all the force of that strong arm—the point of the dagger entering just below the collar-bone and absolutely transfixing the heart. Anthony March was silenced forever!

Then, even as he fell, Pauline's song stopped, and her cry of horror rang through the room. From her seat at the piano she could see what had happened. Is it any wonder that the sight bereft her of her senses?

Macari was standing over his victim. Ceneri was stupefied at the crime which in a moment had obviated any necessity for carrying out his wild plot. The only one who seemed in possession of his wits was Petróff. It was imperative that Pauline should be silenced. Her cries would alarm the neighbours. He rushed forward, and throwing a large woollen sofa-cover over her head, placed her on the couch, where he held her by force.

At that moment I made my frantic entrance—blind and helpless, but, for all they knew, a messenger of vengeance.

Even the ruthless Macari was staggered at my appearance. It was Ceneri who, following the instincts of self-preservation, drew a pistol and cocked it. It was he who understood the meaning of my passionate appeal to their mercy—he who, he averred, saved my life.

Macari, as soon as he recovered from his surprise, insisted that I should share Anthony March's fate. His dagger was once more raised to take human life, whilst Petróff, who had been forced by the new turn of affairs to leave Pauline, pinned me down where I had fallen. Ceneri struck the steel aside and saved me. He examined my eyes and vouched for the truth of my statement. There was no time for recriminations or accusations, but he swore that another murder should not be committed.

Petróff supported him, and Macari at last sullenly yielded, with the stipulation that I should be disposed of in the manner already related. Had the means been at hand I should have been drugged at once; as it was, the old servant, who as yet knew nothing of the tragedy which had taken place, was roused up and sent out in search of the needful draught. The accomplices dared not let me leave their sight, so I was compelled to sit and listen to all their actions.

Why did Ceneri not denounce the murder? Why was he, at least, an accessory after the crime? I can only believe that he was a worse man than he confessed himself to be, or that he trembled at his share in the transaction. After all, he had been planning a crime almost as black, and when the truth as to the trust money was known, no jury in the world would have acquitted him. Perhaps both he and Petróff held human life lightly; their hands were certainly not clean from political assassinations. Feeling that a trial must go hard with them, they threw their lot in with Macari's, and at once set about baffling inquiry and hiding all traces of the crime. From that moment there was little to choose between the degrees in criminality of the three men.

Now that they were all sailing in the same boat, they had little doubt of success. Teresa was perforce taken into their confidence. This was no matter, as, devoted to Ceneri, she would have aided in a dozen murders had her master decreed them. First of all, they must get rid of me. Petróff—for Ceneri would not trust me in Macari's hands—went out and found a belated cab. For a handsome consideration the driver consented to lend it to him for an hour and a half. It was still night, so there was no difficulty in carrying my senseless form to it without observation.

Petróff drove off, and having deposited me in a by-way a long distance from the house, returned the cab to its owner and rejoined his companions.

And now for Pauline. Her moans had gradually died away, and she lay in a death-like stupor. The great danger to the accomplices would be from her. Until she recovered nothing could be done save to carry her to her room and place her under Teresa's charge. When she awoke they must decide what course to pursue.

But the pressing thing was, how to make away with the dead body of the murdered man. All sorts of plans were discussed, until one at last was adopted, the very audacity of which no doubt made it a success. They were now growing desperate and prepared to risk much.

Early in the morning a letter was dispatched to Anthony's lodging, saying that Mr March had been taken seriously ill the night before, and was at his uncle's. This served to stop any inquiry from that quarter. In the meantime the poor young fellow had been laid out as decently as possible, and with everything that could be done to suggest a natural death. A doctor's certificate of death was then forged. Ceneri did not tell me how the form was obtained. The man he got it from knew nothing of its object. An undertaker then was ordered to send a coffin and deal case for the same the next night. The body, in Ceneri's presence, was simply placed inside it, with none of the usual paraphernalia, the reason given for such apparent indecency being that it was only a temporary arrangement, as it was to be taken abroad for interment. The undertaker marvelled, but being well paid, held his peace. Then, by the aid of the forged certificate, the proper formalities were complied with, and in two days' time the three men, in the garb of mourners, were travelling to Italy with the body of their victim. There was nothing to stop them, nothing suspicious in their manner or in the circumstances of the case. They actually took the coffin to the town where Anthony's mother died, and they buried the son by the side of the mother, with his name and the date of his death recorded on the stone. Then they felt safe from everybody except Pauline.

They were safe even from her. When she at last awoke from her stupor, even Teresa could see that something had gone wrong. She said nothing about the scene she had witnessed; she asked no questions. Her past had vanished. According to instructions given her, Teresa, as soon as possible, took her to join Ceneri in Italy, and he saw that Macari's crime had deprived the brother of life and the sister of reason.

No search or inquiry was made for Anthony March. Carrying out his bold plan to the very letter, Ceneri instructed an agent to take possession of his few personal effects at his lodgings, and to inform the people there that he had died at his house and been taken to Italy to be buried with his mother. A few friends for a while regretted a companion, and there was an end of the affair. Nothing having been heard of the blind man, it was supposed he had been wise enough to keep his own counsel.

Months and months passed by, whilst Pauline remained in the same state. Teresa took charge of her, and lived with her in Turin until that time when I saw them at San Giovanni. Ceneri, who had no fixed home, saw little of the girl. His presence did not awaken any painful recollections in her mind, but to him the sight of his niece was unbearable. It recalled what he was eager to forget. She never seemed happy in Italy; in her uncertain way she was pining for England. Anxious to get her out of his sight, he had consented that Teresa should take her to London—had, in fact, come to Turin that particular day to arrange as to their departure. Macari, who, even with a brother's blood between them, considered her in some way his property, accompanied him. He had been continually urging Ceneri to let him marry her, even as she was now. He had threatened to carry her off by force. He had sworn she should be his. She remembered nothing—why should he not wed her?

Bad as Ceneri was, he had recoiled from this. He would even, had it been possible, have broken off all intercourse with Macari; but the men were too deep in each other's secrets to be divided on account of a crime, however atrocious; so he sent Pauline to England. There she was safe from Macari. Then came my proposal, the acceptance of which would take her, at my expense, entirely off his hands and out of his companion's way.

Hence our strange marriage, which even now he justified by saying that should the girl grow attached to anyone, should any feeling corresponding to affection be awakened in her clouded mind, that mind would gradually be built up again.

This, not in his own words, was Ceneri's tale. I now knew all I wanted to know. Perhaps he had painted himself in better colours than he deserved; but he had given me the whole dark history freely and unreservedly, and in spite of the loathing and abhorrence with which he now inspired me, I felt that he had told me the truth.

CHAPTER XIV

DOES SHE REMEMBER?

IT was time to bring our interview to an end. It had lasted
so long that the civil Captain had more than once peeped in
with a significant look on his face, as much as to say there
was such a thing as overstepping the limits of even such an
authority as I held. I had no desire to protract the conversation with the convict. The object of my long journey had
been attained. I had learned all that I could learn. I knew
Pauline's history. The crime had been fully confessed. The
man with me had no claim upon my consideration. Even
had I felt inclined to help him I had no means of so doing.
Why should I linger?

But I did linger for a while. The thought that my rising
and giving the signal that my business was finished would
immediately consign the prisoner to that loathsome den from
which he had emerged was inexpressively painful to me.
Every moment I could keep him with me would be precious
to him. Never again would he see the face of a friend or
acquaintance.

He had ceased speaking. He sat with his head bent forward;
his eyes resting on the ground. A tattered, haggard, hopeless
wretch; so broken down that one dare not reproach him. I
watched him in silence

Presently he spoke: 'You can find no excuse for me, Mr
Vaughan?'

'None,' I said. 'It seems to me there is little to choose
between you and your associates.'

He rose wearily. 'Pauline will recover, you think?'

'I think—I hope I shall find her almost well on my return.'

'You will tell her how you have found me? She may be happier in knowing that Anthony's death has indirectly brought me to this.'

I bowed assent to this dreary request.

'I must go back now,' he said, with a kind of shiver and dragging his weary limbs slowly toward the door.

In spite of his sins I could not let the wretched being go without a word.

'Stop a moment,' l said. 'Tell me if there is anything I can do to make your life any easier?'

He smiled faintly. 'You may give me money—a little. I may be able to keep it and buy a few prisoners' luxuries.'

I gave him several notes which he secreted on his person. 'Will you have more?' I asked. He shook his head.

'I expect these will be stolen from me before I spend them.'

'But is there no way of leaving money with anyone for your use?'

'You might leave some with the Captain. It may be, if he is kind-hearted and honest, a portion of it may reach me. But even that is doubtful.'

I promised to do so, and knew that, whether it reached him or not, I should feel easier for having made the attempt.

'But what will your future be? Where are they taking you, and what will be your life?'

'They are taking us right to the end of Siberia—to Nertchinsk. There I shall be drafted off with others to work in the mines. We go all the way on foot and in chains.'

'What an awful fate!'

Ceneri smiled. 'After what I have passed through, it is Paradise opening before me. When a man offends against the Russian law his one hope is that he may be sent at once to Siberia. That means going from hell to heaven.'

'I do not understand.'

'You would if you had lain like me for months, untried and uncondemned. If you had been placed in a cell without light, without air, without room to move. If you heard those next to you screaming in their madness—madness brought on by solitary confinement and cruel treatment. If every morning as you woke you had said, "I too shall be an idiot before nightfall." If you had been frozen, beaten, starved, in order to make you betray your friends. If you had been reduced to such a state that your death warrant would be welcome; then, Mr Vaughan, you would look forward to and long for the gentle rigours of Siberia. I swear to you sir,' he continued, with more fire and animation than he had yet displayed, 'that if the civilized nations of Europe knew one-tenth part of the horrors and deeds in a Russian prison, they would say, "Guilty or innocent, no human beings shall be tormented like this," and for the sake of common humanity would sweep the whole accursed government from the face of the earth.'

'But twenty years in the mines! Is there no hope of escaping?'

'Where could I escape to? Look at the map and see where Nertchinsk is. If I escaped I could only wander about the mountains until I died or until some of the savages around killed me. No, Mr Vaughan, escapes from Siberia only occur in novels.'

'Then you must slave until your death?'

'I hope not. I once gathered together much information respecting Siberian convicts, and, to tell you the truth, was rather disgusted to find how incorrect the common opinion is. Now I can only hope my researches showed me the truth.'

'The treatment is not so bad, then?'

'It is bad enough, as you are always at the mercy of a petty tyrant. There is no doubt but for a year or two I must slave in the mines. If I survive the toil, which is very unlikely, I may, by finding favour in the ruler's eyes, be released from further work of that description. I may even be allowed to reside at some town and earn my living. I have great hopes that my professional skill may be of use to me. Doctors are scarce in Asiatic Russia.'

Little as he deserved it, my heart echoed his wish; but as I looked at him I felt sure there was small chance of his enduring even a year's toil at the mines.

The door opened and the Captain once more looked in. He was growing quite impatient. I had no reason for wishing to prolong the conversation, so I told him I should have finished in a moment. He nodded his head and withdrew.

'If there is anything more I can do let me know,' I said, turning to Ceneri.

'There is nothing—Stay! one thing. Macari, that villain—sooner or later he will get his deserts. I have suffered—so will he. When that time comes, will you try to send me word? It may be difficult to do so, and I have no right to ask the favour. But you have interest, and might get intelligence sent me. If I am not dead by then, it will make me happier.'

Without waiting for my reply he walked hastily to the door, and with the sentry at his side was marched off to the prison. I followed him.

As the cumbrous lock was being turned he paused. 'Farewell, Mr Vaughan,' he said. 'If I have wronged you I entreat your pardon. We shall meet no more.'

'So far as I am concerned I forgive you freely.'

He hesitated a moment and then held out his hand. The door was now open. I could see the throng of repulsive, villainous faces—the faces of his fellow-prisoners. I could hear the jabber of curiosity and wonder. I could smell the foul odours coming from that reeking den crowded with filthy humanity. And in such a place as this, with such associates, a man of education, culture and refined tastes was doomed to spend his last days. It was a fearful punishment!

Yet it was well merited. As he stood on the threshold with outstretched hand I felt this. To all intents and purposes the man was a murderer. Much moved as I was by his fate I could not bring myself to grasp his hand. My refusal may have been harsh, but I could not do it.

He saw that I did not respond to his action. A flush of shame passed over his face; he bowed his head and turned away. The soldier took him roughly by the arm and thrust him through the doorway. Then he turned, and his eyes met mine with an expression that haunted me for days. He was gazing thus when the heavy door was shut and hid him from my sight for ever.

I turned away sick at heart, perhaps regretting I had added anything to his shame and punishment. I sought my obliging friend, the Captain, and received his word of honour that any money I left with him should be expended for the convict's benefit. I placed a considerable sum in his hands, and can only hope that a part of it reached its destination.

Then I found my interpreter, and ordered horses to be at once procured and the tarantass brought out. I would start without a moment's delay for England—and Pauline!

In half an hour all was ready. Ivan and I stepped into the carriage; the yemschik flourished his whip; the horses sprang forward; the bells jingled merrily, and away we went in the darkness, commencing the return journey which counted by thousands of miles. It was only now, when burning to find myself home again, that I realized the fearful distance which lay between me and my love.

A turn of the road soon hid the gloomy ostrog from my sight, but it was not until we were miles and miles away that my spirits recovered anything like their former tone, and it was days before I ceased to think, at nearly every moment, of that terrible place in which I had found Ceneri, and to which I saw him again consigned after my business with him was finished.

As this is not a book of travel I will not recapitulate the journey. The weather nearly all the time was favourable, the roads were in good condition. My impatience forced me to travel almost day and night. I spared no expense; my extraordinary passport procured me horses when other travellers were compelled to wait—my large gratuities made those horses use their best speed. In thirty-five days we drove up to the Hotel Russia at Nijnei Novgorod, with the tarantass in such a dilapidated condition that in all probability another stage would have finished its work in this world. I bestowed it, a free gift, upon my guide, who, I believe, sold it immediately for three roubles.

From Nijnei by rail to Moscow; from Moscow to St Petersburg. I only tarried in the capital long enough to pay my respects to Lord ——, and once more thank him for his assistance: then, having collected what luggage I had left there, away for England!

On my road from Irkutsk I found letters from Priscilla at Tomsk, at Tobolsk, and at Perm, also more recently written ones at St Petersburg. All up to the date of the last was going on well. Priscilla had taken her charge to Devonshire. Having been reared in that county the old woman had a great belief in its virtues. They were at a quiet but beautiful little watering-place on the north coast, and Priscilla averred that Pauline 'was blooming as a rose and seemed as sensible as Master Gilbert himself'.

No wonder after hearing this good news I was eager to reach home—longing, not only to see my wife again, but to see her, as I had never yet seen her, with her mind restored. Would she remember me? How should we meet? Would she at last learn to love me? Were my troubles at an end or only begun? These were the questions which could only be answered when England was reached.

Home at last! How delightful to stand among one's own countrymen, and hear nothing but good intelligible English around one. I am bronzed with exposure to the wind and sun, my beard has grown to a great length; one or two acquaintances I met when I reached London scarcely knew me. In my present trim I could not hope that I should awaken any recollections in Pauline's mind.

By the aid of a razor and fresh apparel I was soon converted to a fairly good semblance of my former self, and then, without having apprised even Priscilla of my return, I started for the west, to see what fate had in store for me.

What is a run across England after a man has made such a journey as my recent one? Yet that pitiful hundred and fifty miles seemed to me as long as a thousand did a month ago. The last few miles I had to go by coach, and, although four splendid horses spun us along, each individual mile seemed as long as a Siberian stage. But the journey was at last ended, and, leaving my luggage in the coach office, I sallied forth, with a beating heart, to find Pauline.

I went to the address given in Priscilla's letter. The house was a quiet little building, nestling on a wooded bank, with a sloping garden in front, full of late summer flowers. Honeysuckles twined round the porch, great sunflowers stared fiercely from the beds, and carnations sweetened the air. As I waited for the door to be opened I had time to approve Priscilla's choice of a resting place.

I inquired for Mrs Drew. She was not at home—had gone out with the young lady some time ago—and would not be back until the evening. I turned away and went in search of them.

It was early autumn, but the leaf showed no signs of fading. Everything was green, fresh and beautiful. The sky was cloudless, and a soft balmy air fanned my cheek. I paused and looked around me before I decided in which direction to go. Far below my feet lay the little fishing village; its houses clustered round the mouth of the noisy, brawling stream which ran down the valley, and leaped joyously into the sea. On either hand were great tors, and behind them, inland, hills covered with woods, and in front of me stretching away and away was the calm green sea. The scene was fair enough, but I turned away from it. I wanted Pauline.

It seemed to me that on such a day as this the shady woods and the running stream must offer irresistible attractions;

so I found my way down the steep hill, and began walking up the riverside, whilst the merry stream danced past me, throwing its rich brown peat-stained waters into a thousand little cascades as it shot over and foamed round the great boulders which disputed its passage.

I followed its course for about a mile—now clambering over moss-grown rocks, now wading through ferns, now forcing my way through pliant hazel boughs—then in an open space on the opposite bank I saw a girl sitting sketching. Her back was toward me, but I knew every turn of that graceful figure well enough to feel sure she was my wife.

If I had needed extra assurance I had but to look at her companion, who sat near her and appeared to be dozing over a book. I should have recognized that shawl of Priscilla's a mile away—its like has never been known on earth.

Hard as I found it to do so, I resolved not to make my presence known to them. Before I met Pauline I wanted to talk to Priscilla and be guided by her report as to my future method of proceeding. But in spite of my determination I yielded to the temptation of drawing nearer—from where I stood I could not see her face—so I crept on inch by inch till I was nearly opposite the sketcher, and, half hidden by the undergrowth, I stood watching her to my heart's content.

There was the hue of health upon her cheek—there was the appearance of health in every movement, and as she turned and spoke a few words to her companion there was that in her look and in her smile which made my heart bound. The wife I returned to was a different being from the girl I had married.

She turned and looked across the stream. Carried away by my joy I had entirely emerged from my lurking place. With the river between us our eyes met.

She must in some way have remembered me. Were it but as in a dream my face must have seemed familiar to her. She dropped her pencil and sketch-book and sprang to her feet before Priscilla's exclamation of surprise and delight was heard. She stood looking at me as though she expected I would speak or come to her, while the old servant was sending words of welcome across the noisy stream.

Had I wished to retreat, it was now too late. I found a crossing-place and in a minute or two was on the opposite bank.

Pauline had not moved, but Priscilla ran to meet me and almost shook my hands off.

'Does she remember—does she know me?' I whispered, as I disengaged myself and walked toward my wife.

'Not yet; but she will. I am sure she will, Master Gilbert.'

Breathing a prayer that her prophecy might come true, I reached Pauline's side and held out my hand. She took it without hesitation, and raised her dark eyes to mine. How did I refrain from clasping her to my heart?

'Pauline, do you know me?'

She dropped her eyes 'Priscilla has talked of you. She tells me you are a friend and that until you came I must be content and ask no questions.'

'But do you not remember me? I fancied you knew me just now.'

She sighed. 'I have seen you in dreams—strange dreams.' As she spoke a bright blush spread over her cheek.

'Tell me the dreams,' I said.

'I cannot. I have been ill, very ill, for a long time. I have forgotten much—everything that happened.'

'Shall I tell you?'

'Not now—not now.' she cried eagerly. 'Wait, and it may all come back.'

Had she an inkling of the truth? Were the dreams she spoke of but the struggles of growing memory? Did that bright ring which was still on her finger suggest to her what had happened? Yes, I would wait and hope.

We walked back together, with Priscilla following at a proper distance. Pauline seemed to accept my society as though it was a perfectly natural thing to do so. When the path grew steep or rugged she held out her hand for mine, as though its support was her right. Yet for a long time she said nothing.

'Where have you come from?' she asked at last.

'From a long, long journey of many thousands of miles.'

'Yes; when I saw your face you were always travelling. Did you find what you sought?' she asked eagerly.

'Yes. I found the truth. I know everything.'

'Tell me where he is?'

'Where who is?'

'Anthony, my own brother—the boy they killed. Where is his grave?'

'He is buried by the side of his mother.'

'Thank God! I shall be able to pray over him.'

She spoke, if excitedly, quite sensibly, but I wondered she was not craving for justice to be meted out to the murderers.

'Do you wish for vengeance on those who killed him?'

'Vengeance! what good can vengeance do? It will not bring him back to life. It happened long ago. When, I know not; but now it seems years ago. God may have avenged him by now.'

'He has, in a great measure. One died in prison raving mad; another is in chains, working like a slave; the third, as yet, is unpunished.'

'It will come to him, sooner or later. Which is it?'

'Macari.'

She shuddered at the name and said no more. Just before we reached the house in which they lodged, she said, softly and beseechingly, 'You will take me to Italy—to his grave?'

I promised, only too glad to find how instinctively she turned to me to prefer the request. She must remember more than she gave herself credit for.

'I will go there,' she said, 'and see the place, and then we will speak of the past no more.'

We were now at the garden gate. I took her hand in mine.

'Pauline,' I said, 'try—try to remember me.'

A ghost of the old puzzled look came into her eyes; she passed her disengaged hand over her forehead, and then, without a word, turned away and entered the house.

CHAPTER XV

FROM GRIEF TO JOY

My tale is drawing to an end, although I could, for my own pleasure, write chapter after chapter, detailing every occurrence of the next month—describing every look, repeating every word that passed between Pauline and myself, but if I wrote them they would be sacred from all persons save two—my wife and myself.

If my situation was an anomalous one it had at least a certain charm. It was a new wooing, none the less entertaining and sweet because its object happened to be already my wife in name. It was like a landowner walking over his estate and in every direction finding unsuspected beauties and unknown mines of wealth. Every day showed me fresh charms in the woman I loved.

Her smile was a joy greater than I had ever pictured, her laugh a revelation. To gaze into those bright unclouded eyes and strive to learn their secrets was a reward that repaid me for all that I suffered. To find that her intellect, now restored, was fit to be matched with anyone's—to know that when the time came I should be given not only a wife, beautiful in my eyes above all women, but a companion and a sympathetic friend—how can I describe my rapture?

Yet it was a rapture not unmodified by doubts and fears. It may be that my character lacked that very useful trait called by some self-confidence and by others conceit. The more I saw to love and admire in Pauline, the more I asked myself how I could dare to expect that so peerless a creature would condescend to accept the love and the life I wished to offer her. Who was I to win her? I was rich, it is true, but I felt sure that riches would not buy her affection—besides, as I had not told her that her own wealth was swept away, she fancied her fortune was as large as my own. She was young, beautiful, and, so far as she knew, free and amply provided for. No, I had nothing to offer her which was worthy of her acceptance.

I quite dreaded to look forward to the moment which must sooner or later come—the moment when I must, ignoring the past, ask her once more to be my wife. On her answer would hang the whole of my future life. No wonder I decided to postpone the ordeal until I felt quite certain that the result of it would be favourable to me. No wonder that when with Pauline, and realizing the value of the prize I aimed at, I grew quite humble and depreciatory of what merits I may have possessed. No wonder that at times I wished that I were gifted with that pleasing assurance which sits so well on many men, and, time and opportunity being given, seems to go a long way toward winning a woman's heart.

Time and opportunity at least were not wanting in my case.

I had taken up my quarters near to her, and from morn to night we were in each other's company. We wandered through the narrow Devonshire lanes, with the luxuriant banks of ferns on either side. We climbed the rugged tors. We fished with more or less success the rapid streams. We drove together. We read and sketched—but as yet we had not talked of love; though all the while my wedding-ring was on her finger.

It required all my authority to prevent Priscilla telling Pauline the truth. On this point I was firm. Unless the past came back of its own accord, I would hear her say she loved me before my lips revealed it to her. Perhaps it was the idea which at times came to me, that Pauline remembered more than she would own to, kept me steadfast in this resolution.

It was curious the way in which she at once fell into friendly, unconstrained intercourse with me. We might have known each other from childhood, so perfectly natural and unembarrassed was her manner when we were together. She made no demur when I begged her to call me by my Christian name, nor did she object to my making use of her own. Had she done so I cannot think in what form I should have addressed her. Although I had instructed Priscilla to call her Miss March, the old woman stoutly objected to this, and compounded matters by speaking to her and of her as Miss Pauline.

The days slipped by—the happiest days my life had as yet known. Morn, noon and eve we were together; and I fear were objects of great curiosity to our neighbours, who no doubt wondered what relation existed between me and the beautiful girl at whose side I ever was.

I soon found that Pauline's natural disposition was gay and bright. It was too soon yet to expect it to reassert itself, yet I was not without hopes that before long that look, telling of sad memories, which so often crossed her face, would fade away forever. Now and again a pleased smile lit up her face, and merry words slipped from her lips. Although, when reason first returned to her, it seemed as if her brother's death had occurred but the day before, I felt sure that, after a while, she understood that years had passed since the fatal night. These years were to her wrapped in a mist; they seemed as dreams. She was trying to recall them, beginning at the beginning; and I need not say with what alacrity I lent my aid.

By common consent we avoided the future, but of the past, or all the past in which I was not concerned, we spoke freely. All the events of her early years she now remembered perfectly; she could account for everything up to the time when her brother was struck down—after that came mistiness; from which she emerged to find herself in a strange room, ill, and being nursed by a strange nurse.

Several days passed before Pauline questioned me as to the part I had played in her clouded life. One evening we stood on the top of a thickly wooded hill, from which we could just catch a glimpse of the sea, now reddened by a glorious sunset. We had been silent for some time, and who can say that our thoughts were not more in unison than any words we could have spoken while our strange and uncertain relations continued. I looked at the western sky until the glowing tints began to fade, then turning to my companion I found her dark eyes gazing at me with almost painful earnestness.

'Tell me,' she said, 'tell me what I shall find when that lost time comes back to me?'

Her fingers, as she spoke, were playing with her wedding ring. She still wore it, and the diamond keeper I had placed above it; but she had not as yet asked me why it was on her hand.

'Will it come back, Pauline, do you think?' I asked.

'I hope so—or should I hope so? Tell me, will it bring me joy or sorrow?'

'Who can say—the two are always mingled.'

She sighed and turned her eyes to the ground. Presently she raised them to mine.

'Tell me,' she said, 'how and when did you come into my life—why did I dream of you?'

'You saw me so often when you were ill.'

'Why did I wake and find your old servant taking care of me?'

'Your uncle gave you into my charge. I promised to watch over you during his absence.'

'And he will never return. He is punished for his crime—for standing by when the poor boy was murdered.'

She pressed her hands to her eyes, as if to shut out the light.

'Pauline,' I said, wishing to change the current of her thoughts, 'tell me how you saw me in dreams; what you dreamed of me?'

She shuddered. 'I dreamed that you were standing by me—in the very room—that you saw the deed. Yet I knew that it could not be so.'

'And then?'

'I saw your face many times—it was always travelling, travelling through clouds. I saw your lips move and you seemed to say, 'I am going to learn the truth—so I waited patiently till you returned.'

'You never dreamed of me before?'

It was growing dusk. I was uncertain whether it was the deepening shade from the trees which made her cheeks look darker, or whether it was a blush. My heart was beating madly.

'I cannot tell! I don't know! Don't ask me!' she said in a troubled voice. Then she turned. 'It grows dark and chilly. Let us go in.'

I followed her. It was so completely the rule for me to spend the evening with her that I did not even wait for an invitation. It was our custom to play and sing together for an hour or two. Pauline's first expressed desire after her recovery had been for a piano. Believing herself to be an heiress she had felt no scruple in asking for all she wanted, and my instructions to Priscilla being that no money was to be spared in ministering to her comforts, a piano had been sent from the nearest town.

All her skill had returned to her. Her voice had come back even stronger and more sweet than of old. Again and again she held me entranced as she had held me once before, when I little expected the fearful ending to her song, or that my fate and the singer's were so closely interwoven.

I was surprised, therefore, when this evening she turned on the doorstep and said, 'Not tonight. Leave me, please, for tonight.'

I urged no objection. I took her hand and bade her farewell until the morrow. I would go and wander by starlight and think of her.

As we parted she looked at me strangely, almost solemnly.

'Gilbert,' she said, speaking in Italian; for Priscilla was now standing at the open door—'shall I pray for the past to return or that I should never remember it? Which will be the best for me—and for you?'

Without waiting to hear my reply, she glided past Priscilla, who stood waiting for me to follow her.

'Good night, Priscilla,' I said, 'I am not coming in.'

'Not coming in, Master Gilbert! Miss Pauline will be vexed.'

'She is tired and not quite well. You had better go to her. Good night.'

Priscilla came out to the doorstep and closed the door behind her. There was something in her manner which told me she meant on this particular occasion to resume what she could of that authority she had been delegated to exercise over me during my tender years—an authority I did not dare to dispute until long after I had been invested with jackets and trousers. I have no doubt but she would have liked to have seized me by the collar and given me a sound shaking. As it was she was obliged to content herself with throwing a world of sorrowful indignation into her voice.

'She may easily feel ill, poor young lady, when her husband lives at one house and she at another, and here's everybody round about trying to find what relation you two are to each other—asking me all sorts of questions, and I mustn't say you are husband and wife.'

'No—not yet.'

'Well, I am going to, Master Gilbert. If you won't tell the poor young lady, I shall. I'll tell her how you brought her home and sent for me to take care of her—how you tended her and waited on her all day long—how you shut yourself up for her sake, never seeing an old friend's face. Oh, yes, Master Gilbert, I'll tell her all; and I'll tell her how you went into her room and kissed her ere you started on that fool's journey, wherever it was. She'll remember everything fast enough then.'

'I command you to say nothing.'

'I've heeded too many commands of yours, Master Gilbert, to mind breaking one for your sake. I'll do it and take the consequences.'

Feeling that the explanation, if made by Priscilla, would not only sweep away a great deal of romance, but also might precipitate matters and make them far more difficult to adjust to my own satisfaction, I was bound to prevent her carrying out her threat. Knowing from old experience that although the good soul could not be driven, she could be led, I was obliged to resort to cajolery. So I said, as one asking a boon—

'You won't if I entreat and beg you not to, my old friend. You love me too much to do anything against my wishes.'

Priscilla was not proof against this appeal, but she urged me to proclaim the true state of affairs as soon as possible.

'And don't be too sure, Master Gilbert,' she concluded, 'as to what she remembers or doesn't. Sometimes I think she knows a good deal more than you suppose.'

Then she left me, and I went wandering about, thinking as to what meaning to attach to Pauline's parting words.

'Which will be the best for me—and for you?'—to forget or to recall? How much did she forget—how much did she recall? Had those rings on her hand not shown her that she was a wife? Could she help suspecting whose wife she was? Even if she remembered nothing about our strange hurried marriage, nothing about our subsequent life together, she found herself after that interval of oblivion, as it were, under my charge; found that I knew all the tragic circumstances of her brother's end, that I had now returned from a journey of thousands of miles, undertaken to learn the fatal particulars. Although she might not be able to account for it, she must by this time know the truth. Keeping the ring on her finger showed that she did not dispute the fact that, somehow, she was wedded. Who could be her husband except me?

Yes, by the evidence the situation offered, I determined that she had arrived at the right conclusion; and the hour was at hand when I should learn if the knowledge would bring her joy or sorrow.

Tomorrow I would tell her all. I would tell her how strangely our lives became linked. I would plead for her love more passionately than ever man yet pleaded. I would prove to her how innocently I had fallen into Ceneri's schemes, how free from blame I was in wedding her whilst her mental state was such that she was unable to refuse consent. All this she should learn, and then I would hear my doom from her lips.

I would urge no plea based upon my legal right to my wife. So far as I could make her she should be free. Nothing should bind her to me except love. If she had none to give me, I would tear myself from her, and at her wish see if steps could not be taken to annul the marriage—but whether she elected to remain my wife in name, to become my wife in reality, or to sever every tie, her future life, with or without her knowledge, should be my care. By this time tomorrow my fate should be known.

Having settled this I should have retired to rest, but I was in no mood for sleep. Again and again I recalled her last words and commenced one of those weighings of hopes and fears which always means self-torture. Why, if Pauline had guessed the truth, had she not asked me about it? How could she spend hour after hour with me, knowing she was my wife yet not knowing how she became so? Would her words admit of the interpretation that she dreaded what she had to learn? Did she wish for freedom and continual forgetfulness? So, on and on until I made myself quite miserable.

Many a man on the eve of learning whether his love is to be accepted or rejected has been racked as I was that night, but surely no lover save myself ever lived, who was to receive the momentous answer from the lips of a woman who was already his wife.

The hour was late when I returned from my solitary walk. I passed Pauline's window and standing gazing up at it I wondered if she, too, were lying awake and thinking and deciding about our future lives. Ah well, tomorrow would put us both out of suspense!

The night being still and warm her window was open at the top. Before I turned away a fancy seized me. I picked a rose from a bush in the garden and managed to toss it through the open sash. She might find it in the morning, and guessing from whom it came might wear it. It would be a good omen.

The blind shivered as the rosebud struck it: then, fearing discovery, I turned and fled.

The morning broke fair. I rose with hope in my heart and scouted the fears of the night. At the earliest moment I could hope to find her I started in search of Pauline. She had just gone out. I ascertained in which way and followed her.

I found her walking slowly, with her head bent. She greeted me with her usual quiet sweetness, and we walked on side by side. I looked in vain for my rose; and was fain to comfort myself by thinking it must have fallen where she could not see it. Nevertheless, I was troubled.

And there was worse in store for me. Her hands, ungloved and with the fingers interlaced, were carried in front of her. I was walking on her left side, and I saw that the hand nearest me was denuded of its rings. The golden circlet which had shone until now like a beacon of hope, had disappeared. My heart sank. The meaning was only too clear: when coupled with her words of last night, who could fail to understand it? Although she knew herself to be my wife she wished to throw the yoke aside. Pauline loved me not—the truth which was gradually creeping from the misty past would bring her sorrow—now that she remembered, she wished to forget. The rings were cast aside to show me, if possible, without words, that she was not to be my wife.

How could I speak now? The answer had been given before the question had been put.

She saw me looking at that little white hand of hers, but simply dropped her lashes and said nothing. No doubt she wished me to spare her the pain of an explanation. If I could nerve myself to it, perhaps the best thing would be to leave her as speedily as possible—leave her to return no more.

Moody and despondent as I felt at the discovery just made, it was not long before I found a great change in Pauline's manner. She was not the same. Something had come between us, something which entirely dispelled the old friendly intercourse; changing it into little more than conventional politeness. Shyness and restraint now made themselves manifest in every word and action—perhaps in mine also. We spent the day together as usual, but the companionship must have been irksome to both, so greatly was its footing changed for the worse. That night I went to bed wretched. The prize I had striven for seemed to be snatched away just as I had hoped to win it!

So several days passed. Pauline made no sign, or certainly none I could construe favourably. I could bear this state of things no longer. Priscilla, whose sharp eyes saw that something was amiss, pestered me beyond endurance; and spoke her mind so roundly that I began to suspect she had already executed her threat of telling Pauline everything; and I felt inclined to attribute my failure to the old woman's officiousness in making a premature revelation. All might have gone well had I been given another week or a fortnight to win my wife's heart. I began to believe that she was growing unhappy; that my presence troubled her. Not that she evinced any wish to avoid me; indeed, she came so surely at my beck and call as to suggest a shadow of the obedience she had always given during those days upon which I now dreaded to dwell. But I felt she would be happier and more at ease in my absence. So I resolved to depart.

I knew that my only way was to carry out my determination at once. Having made the resolve, I would act upon it next day. I packed up my things in readiness. I arranged by which coach to go. I should have three hours in the morning to give Priscilla my final instructions and to bid my wife adieu forever.

I could not go without explaining some things to her. I need not pain her by alluding to our relationship, but I must inform her that she was not the heiress she believed. I must tell her she had plenty to live upon without saying that I, her husband, would supply it. When this was arranged, farewell for ever!

As soon as I had finished my pretence at a breakfast, I walked across to the house where Pauline lodged. As yet she knew nothing of my purpose. I held her hand rather longer than usual, and by a desperate effort forced words to my lips.

'I am come to say goodbye. I go to London today.'

She answered not a word, but I felt her hand tremble in my own. Her eyes I could not see.

'Yes, I have loitered here long enough,' I continued, attempting to speak easily, 'a great many things call me to town.'

Pauline was not looking in the best of health this morning Her cheek was paler than it had been since my arrival. She looked languid and depressed. Doubtless my presence had worried her. Poor girl, she would soon be relieved of that!

Seeing that I paused for her to speak she found her voice, but even that seemed to have lost some of its freshness and tone.

'When do you go?' was all she said. Not a word about my return!

'By the midday coach. I have still some hours left. As it is the last time, shall we walk to the Clearing together?'

'Do you wish it?'

'If you have no objection. Besides, I want to speak to you about yourself—about business matters,' I added, to show that she need not fear the interview.

'I will come,' she said, quitting the room hurriedly.

I waited. Presently Priscilla appeared. She was looking daggers at me—undeserved, at least from her. Her voice was harsh and raspy, bringing back to my mind a familiar sound of early childhood, when I had committed some petty crime which excited her ire.

'Miss Pauline begs you will walk on and not wait for her. She will join you at the Clearing presently.'

I took my hat and prepared to do as commanded. Priscilla had said nothing which showed she knew of my approaching departure, but as I was passing out of the house she said, in a tone of withering scorn, 'Master Gilbert, you're a bigger fool than I thought you were.'

Such an observation, even from an old servant, could not be passed by. I turned to remonstrate. Priscilla simply slammed the door almost against my nose.

I walked away—the thing in the face of my other troubles was not worth a thought. Of course I could not expect Priscilla to enter into my feelings and appreciate the delicacy of my position. Besides, I must see her and have a long talk with her before I left.

The Clearing, as we called it, was a place on the hillside, not far away. We had stumbled upon it, almost by accident, during our walks. A seldom-trodden path through the wood led to a spot from which the trees and undergrowth had been cleared. From it there was a delightful view of the opposite hills and the stream winding through the valley. It was a favourite resort of mine. Here I had sat for hours talking to Pauline and here in my dreams I had poured forth the words of love I longed to speak—and here I was to say goodbye forever!

My frame of mind was a sad one when I reached the Clearing. I threw myself down on the sloping ground and turned my eyes up the path by which she must come. A fallen trunk at my back formed a rest for my head—the trees around were rustling in the soft breeze—the monotonous rush of the stream below was soothing and lulling—a few white clouds sailed slowly across the sky. It was a drowsy, dreamy, beautiful morning. I had scarcely slept for the last two or three nights. Pauline lingered. Is it any wonder that my eyes closed and for a while all sorrow and disappointment were chased away by the sleep I so sorely needed?

Was it sleep? Yes, because one must sleep in order to dream. Ah! if that dream were reality, life would be worth having. I dreamed that my wife was beside me, that she took my hand and pressed her lips to it passionately, that her cheek was almost touching mine, that I could feel her soft, sweet breath. So real did it seem that I turned on my hard rustic pillow towards the dream, and then of course it vanished.

I opened my eyes. In front of me stood Pauline. Those grand dark eyes of hers no longer veiled by the lashes, but open and looking into mine. I saw them but for a second, but that was long enough for the look I had surprised to send the blood throbbing through my veins—to make me spring to my feet—to embolden me to take her suddenly and swiftly in my arms—to cover her sweet face with kisses, ejaculating the only words that one can find at such a time, 'I love you! I love you! I love you!'

For no man yet has seen in a woman's eyes the look I saw in Pauline's unless that woman loves him above all the world.

No words can describe the rapture of that moment—the revulsion of my feelings. She was mine, my own forever. I knew it; I could feel it every time my lips touched hers. The bright blush which spread from her cheek to her neck proclaimed it—her suffering without resistance my passionate caresses confirmed it—but let me hear it from those sweet lips!

'Pauline! Pauline!' I cried; 'do you love me?'

A trembling which I knew was of joy passed over her.

'Do I love you! love you!' she said, and hid her blushing face on my shoulder. The words, the action, was enough, but presently she raised her head and pressed her lips to mine.

'I love you—yes, I love you, my husband!'

'When did you know? When did you remember?'

For a moment she answered not. She broke from my embrace; then, opening the bosom of her dress, drew forth a blue ribbon which hung round her neck. Upon it were threaded the two rings. They seemed to sparkle with joy in the bright sun.

She detached them and held them towards me. 'Gilbert, my love, my husband, if you will that I shall be your wife, if you think me worthy of it, take them and place them where they should be.'

And then once more, with many a kiss, many a vow, I placed the rings upon her finger and knew that my troubles were at an end.

'But when did you know—when did the memory come back?'

'Dearest,' she whispered, and her voice sounded like music, 'I knew it when I saw you standing on the river bank. It came to me all at once. Till then all was dark. I saw your face and knew everything.'

'Why did you not tell me?'

She hung her head. 'I wanted to find out if you loved me. Why should you do so? If you did not we could part, and I would set you free if possible. But not now, Gilbert; you will never get rid of me now.'

Her thoughts had been the same as mine. No wonder I had misunderstood her. The idea of her waiting to see if I loved her seemed so preposterous!

'You would have saved me days of grief if I had known you cared for me. Why did you take off the rings, Pauline?'

'Day after day passed and you said nothing. Then I took them off. They have been next to my heart ever since, waiting for you to give back when you chose.'

I kissed the hand on which they shone. 'Then all is clear to you now, my own wife?'

'Not quite all, but enough. The truth, the love, the devotion—all this, my husband, I can remember—all this I will repay, if my love can do it.'

Our wooing may close with these words—let all the rest be sacred. The trees around alone know what passed between us, as their kindly shade fell on us where we sat and interchanged our words of love whilst hour after hour of our second and real wedding day slipped by. At last we rose, but lingered yet awhile, as though loath to leave the spot where happiness had come to us. We looked round once more and bid farewell to hill and valley and stream: we gazed long in each other's eyes, our lips met again in a passionate kiss; then we went forth together to the world and the new sweet life awaiting us.

We walked as in a dream, from which we were only recalled by the sight of houses and people.

'Pauline!' I whispered, 'can you leave this place tonight? We will go to London.'

'And afterwards?' she asked, wistfully.

'Can you ask me? To Italy, of course.'

She thanked me with a look and pressure of her hand. We were now at her home. She left me, passing Priscilla, whose honest eyes were glowering at me. Priscilla had called me a fool; I must be revenged.

'Priscilla,' I said gravely, 'I am going by this evening's coach. I will write when I get to London.'

I had my revenge in full. The good old soul almost fell weeping at my feet.

'Oh, Master Gilbert, don'tee, don'tee go, sir! That poor young lady, Miss Pauline, what will she do? She loves the very ground you tread upon.'

I had bargained for reproaches, not sentiment of this kind. I laid my hand upon her shoulder.

'But, Priscilla, Miss Pauline—Mrs Vaughan, my wife, goes with me.'

Priscilla's tears came more copiously than before, but they were tears of joy.

Ten days later and Pauline stood by her brother's grave. By her own wish she visited it alone. I waited at the gate of the cemetery until she rejoined me. Her face was very pale, her eyes showed traces of many tears, but she smiled as she met my anxious glance.

'Gilbert, my husband,' she said, 'I have wept, but now I smile. The past is the past. Let its darkness be dispersed by the brightness of the present and the promise of the future. Let the love I bore my brother be carried into the greater love I give my husband. Let us turn our backs on the dark shadows and begin our lives.'

Have I more to tell? One thing only.

Years afterwards I was in Paris. The great war had been fought out to the bitter end. Traces of the conflict between the two races had almost vanished, but those of the second and internecine contest were visible everywhere. The Gaul himself had destroyed what the Teuton spared. The Tuileries, with sightless, empty eyes, gazed sadly toward the Place de la Concord, where stood the statues of the fair lost provinces. The Vendôme column lay prostrate. The fair city was charred and blackened by the incendiary torches of her own sons; but the flames had been some time extinguished and ample revenge had been taken. A gay young officer, a friend of mine, took me to see a military prison. We were chatting and smoking in the open air when a small body of soldiers appeared. They were escorting three men, who walked with fettered hands and bowed heads.

'Who are they?' I asked.

'Blackguard Communists.'

'Where are they taking them?'

The Frenchmen shrugged his shoulders. 'Where they ought all to be taken—to be shot, the brutes!'

Brutes or not, three men who have but a minute to live must be objects of interest, if not sympathy. I looked closely at them as they passed us. One of them raised his head and stared me in the face. It was Macari!

I started as his eyes met mine, but I am not ashamed to say the movement was caused by no feeling of compassion. Ceneri, in spite of myself, I pitied, and would have aided had it been possible, but this ruffian, liar and traitor should have gone to his doom, even if I could have saved him by lifting a finger. He had passed long ago out of my life, but my blood still boiled when I thought of him and his crimes. I knew not how he had lived since I last saw him—knew not whom or how many he had betrayed; but if Justice had been slow in claiming him, her sword had at last reached him and his end was close at hand.

He knew me—perhaps he thought I had come there to gloat over his punishment. A look of bitter hate crossed his face. He stopped and cursed me. The guard forced him on. He turned his head and cursed me until one of the soldiers smote him on the mouth. The action may have been cruel, but there was little mercy shown to Communists in those days. The guard and their prisoners turned round an angle of the building.

'Shall we see the end?' said my friend, flipping the ash off his cigar.

'No, thank you.'

But we heard it. In ten minutes the rattle of rifles sounded, and I knew that the last and the guiltiest of Anthony March's murderers had found his deserts.

I remembered my promise to Ceneri. With great trouble I managed to get a message sent which I believed would reach him. Six months afterwards a letter stamped with innumerable hieroglyphical postmarks was delivered to me. It told me that the prisoner to whom I had written had died two years after his arrival at the mines. So the lesser criminal had not the satisfaction of knowing the fate of the man who had betrayed him.

My tale is told. My life and Pauline's began when we turned from the cemetery and resolved to forget the past. Since then our joys and griefs have been the same as those of thousands. As I write this in my happy country house, blessed with wife and children, I wonder if I could ever have been that blind man who heard those fearful sounds and who saw afterwards that terrible sight. Could it have been I who rushed from one end of Europe to the other to set at rest a doubt which I blush at even harbouring? Could it have been Pauline, whose eyes now shine with love and intelligence, who lay for months, even years, with the sweet bells of her intellect jangled and out of tune?

Yes, it must be so; for she has read every line I have written, and as we peruse and revise this last page her arm steals round me, and she says, insisting that I shall record her utterance:

'Too much, too much of me, my husband, not enough of what you did and have always done for me!'

With this, the only difference of opinion that exists between us, my tale may end.

THE END

THE DETECTIVE
STORY CLUB

FOR DETECTIVE
CONNOISSEURS

recommends

"The Man with the Gun."

MR. BALDWIN'S FAVOURITE

THE LEAVENWORTH
CASE   *By* ANNA K. GREEN

THIS exciting detective story, published towards the end of
last century, enjoyed an enormous success both in England
and America. It seems to have been forgotten for nearly fifty years
until Mr. Baldwin, speaking at a dinner of the American Society
in London, remarked : " An American woman, a successor of Poe,
Anna K. Green, gave us *The Leavenworth Case*, which I still think
one of the best detective stories ever written." It is a remarkably
clever story, a masterpiece of its kind, and in addition to an exciting
murder mystery and the subsequent tracking down of the criminal,
the writing and characterisation are excellent. *The Leavenworth Case*
will not only grip the attention of the reader from beginning to end
but will also be read again and again with increasing pleasure.

CALLED BACK

By HUGH CONWAY

BY the purest of accidents a man who is blind accidentally comes
on the scene of a murder. He cannot see what is happening,
but he can hear. He is seen by the assassin who, on discovering
him to be blind, allows him to go without harming him. Soon afterwards he recovers his sight and falls in love with a mysterious
woman who is in some way involved in the crime. . . . The mystery
deepens, and only after a series of memorable thrills is the tangled
skein unravelled.

LOOK FOR THE MAN WITH THE GUN